BOG

BOG

KAREN KROSSING

Fitzhenry & Whiteside

Published in Canada by Fitzhenry & Whiteside, 195 Allstate Parkway, Markham, Ontario L3R 4T8
Published in the United States by Fitzhenry & Whiteside, 311 Washington Street, Brighton, Massachusetts 02135

www.fitzhenry.ca   godwit@fitzhenry.ca

10 9 8 7 6 5 4 3 2 1

Library and Archives Canada Cataloguing in Publication
Bog
ISBN 978-1-55455-315-0 (Paperback) | 978-1-55455-871-1 (ePub) | 978-1-55455-870-4 (ePDF)
Data available on file

Publisher Cataloging-in-Publication Data (U.S.)
Bog
ISBN 978-1-55455-315-0 (Paperback) | 978-1-55455-871-1 (ePub) | 978-1-55455-870-4 (ePDF)
Data available on file

Fitzhenry & Whiteside acknowledges with thanks the Canada Council for the Arts, and the Ontario Arts Council for their support of our publishing program. We acknowledge the financial support of the Government of Canada through the Canada Book Fund (CBF) for our publishing activities.

Cover and interior design by Daniel Choi
Cover illustration by Félix Girard

Printed in Canada

For trolls everywhere

1

STONE

BOG smelled the humans from across the lake. The stench floated high on the breeze, infecting the stars themselves, and then settled among the branches of the birch trees. What were humans doing in their hunting grounds?

Wrinkling his nose, Bog trailed his father, Jeddal, through the undergrowth. Jeddal twitched his tail, jerking its feathery plume from side to side. Bog flicked his own blunt tail, too.

Silent as stone, they increased the distance between them and the source of the smell. Not a twig cracked under their bare feet. Not a leaf fluttered as they passed. The darkness cloaked them, and their night vision shielded them from a surprise attack by bumbling humans.

"Never hunt a human, Bog." Jeddal's growl was barely audible.

Bog nodded at the familiar lesson. "They're not even good enough for the stewpot," he whispered.

They trekked through the forest under the canopy of stars that winked off and on through the trees. When a flying squirrel glided onto a nearby branch, Bog crouched, ready to spring. He could already smell roasted squirrel turning on a spit.

"Leave it." Jeddal grunted. "They're still too close."

Bog's stomach grumbled, but he obeyed.

They walked until the moon rose above the treetops. It was half-full, gleaming silver against a deep purple sky.

"Why are they here?" Bog asked once they were far from the weak human ears. "I thought they slept at night."

Jeddal scowled. "Who knows?" He led Bog toward a colossal rock formation—Ymir's bones rising out of the earth. In a darkened hollow on its eastern side, Jeddal stopped, lowering his rucksack. "Humans aren't very smart, so much of what they do doesn't make sense." He pulled out a jug of broth, uncorked it, and hoisted it to his lips.

Even in the shadows, Jeddal's grey pelt was magnificent, his prodigious nose impressive. Bog glanced down at his own leathery hide that showed through his patchy grey fur. With a blunt nose and no fur on his face, hands, and feet, he wasn't much of a troll, although he tried to be a good son.

Jeddal passed the jug to Bog. "I used to believe trolls and humans could live in peace, even after a human killed my father. But no more."

Jeddal had never talked about peace before.

"What happened?"

"I trusted a human. One foolish time." Jeddal's eyes became unfocused, as if he were recalling some distant memory from the black undergrowth of his mind.

"Which human?" Bog prodded for more.

Jeddal waved his question away. "Once they get your scent, humans will hound you."

"Because they only cause trouble?" Bog took a swig and then recorked the jug. The broth was cold, a tasty leftover from the night's breakfast with Kasha and the youngsters.

"That's right," Jeddal muttered. "They'll kill for revenge. Or even for sport. I once saw some humans kill a moose and then take the head for a trophy."

Bog licked his lips. "What did they do with all that meat?"

"They left it." Jeddal took the jug from him.

"But why—"

"Enough questions." Jeddal shoved the jug into his rucksack. "We've hunting to do. The youngsters can't feed themselves."

A twig snapped in the distance, beyond the rock formation. The human stench invaded once again, drifting from the abandoned deer track he and Jeddal had just trekked.

"Are *they* hunting *us*?" Bog whispered.

Jeddal wiggled his ears, listening intently. "If these humans want a trail to follow, we'll give them one." He headed away from the cave where Kasha and the youngsters would be going about their chores, unsuspecting.

"Break branches, Bog. Step heavy. Make it easy for them to track us," Jeddal ordered, not bothering to lower his voice. "It's going to be a long walk for those humans."

For us, too, thought Bog, but he said nothing.

The reek and noise of the humans trailed them endlessly as Jeddal led them northwest, farther and farther from the family cave.

Halfway through the night, when Bog's legs demanded a rest, he asked, "Why not fight the humans, Father? I only scent two—we could be done with them quickly. Then we could hunt a juicy, plump raccoon or a—"

"We'd have more humans after us by next nightfall." Jeddal's tail whipped the nearby branches. "And then what would we do—fight them all? No, a cunning troll lives to see the moon rise."

Bog plodded after Jeddal, stomping a path for the stupid humans to find. Of course, his father was right. If only the humans didn't alert the squirrels and other prey wherever they went. Ridding their forest of humans was hungry work.

Jeddal's trail ended at a distant swamp, teeming with mosquitoes to sting the humans' feeble hide and thick with mud to ensnare their feet. Once they lost the humans in the worst of the ooze, Bog and Jeddal headed back, quiet as starlight, hiding their trail by wading through a shallow stream.

It was a clever plan, even if it was tiring.

By the time the darkness faded and the sun threatened to rise above the treetops, only six deer mice swung by their tails from Bog's fist, with nothing else in his rucksack.

Bog hurried after Jeddal, slipping through the shadows that still clung to the rocks and clumped under the thick fir trees. The early morning glow of the sky stung his eyes.

"Odin's curse," he said, hating the sun's power, its ability to turn them to stone.

They scurried across a clearing littered with fist-sized rocks, crouching boulders, and low bushes of juniper and blueberry. Almost to the family cave. Kasha and the youngsters would be anxious for their safe arrival.

The humans' scent still wafted on the breeze from behind; they must have passed this way earlier in the night—only about a thousand paces from the cave. Dangerously close.

Bog squinted against the growing light, just as a thin old man and a fat shorter one emerged from a stand of scrawny cedars. He snarled, dropping the night's catch in a lifeless heap, but Jeddal cowered, kicking a sideways warning at him. *Never let humans know how smart you are.* Bog let his jaw hang open, eyes glaze over, and spit drool over his lip.

"Don't hurt us," Jeddal pleaded in the human tongue, his voice thick and slow, his tail drooping. Jeddal was a head taller than the thin man, who was a head taller than Bog.

"What did I tell you?" the fat man said. "As big as a boulder, as dumb as a cow." He aimed a rock at Bog—too far to the left.

Bog slid sideways so the misfired rock hit his chest. "Ooof." He dropped one shoulder in mock pain.

The humans sniggered.

Bog caught the scent of a third human. A scrawny young thing—barely a man—had sneaked toward the clearing through a hollow rich with ferns. Bog kept a wary eye on him, even though he was too puny to do much damage.

"Please, spare us," Jeddal begged as he edged closer to a boulder the size of a beaver—a good choice for throwing. "We have great riches and magic. Gold, silver, and a pot that never empties of hearty stew."

As if they had such a pot. Bog remembered to hunch, low and weak, keeping one eye on Jeddal. They'd have to fight now—no time for trickery before sunrise.

"Don't try to fool me, you no-soul. I haven't chased you all night just to get your baubles or your pot."

The thin man strutted between Jeddal and the boulder, oblivious to his upcoming fate.

The fat man hurled another rock. This time it hit Jeddal, who whimpered, even though he had a thick hide that not even a human's gunshot could pierce.

"I can't trick you, wise human." Jeddal bowed his head, exposing the back of his furry neck.

Although his knees wanted to buckle, Bog stayed crouched, silently urging the thin man to stop blocking Jeddal's way to the boulder.

"Tell us where your cave is and we'll let you go." The thin man swatted the mosquitoes that easily penetrated his flesh. All three humans were covered in cloth, as if their fur and hide weren't enough.

"Why do you want my cave?" Jeddal glanced up, his eyebrows crumpled together like he didn't understand.

The fat man held up another rock. Bog whimpered and hunched his shoulders as he checked that the puny human hadn't moved.

"I said, tell us where it is," the thin man demanded, finally pacing closer to Bog, leaving the boulder exposed. "Are you hiding others? Where are the rest of the trolls, you useless, stupid creatures?"

Bog let a growl escape. Long before humans existed, trolls had sprouted from the feet of the mighty frost giant Ymir. Trolls would rule the mountains, lakes, and forests long after humans were gone.

"Please, no more rocks. I'll show you to my cave."

Jeddal went down on one knee, close enough to reach the boulder now, his knuckles scraping the ground.

The thin man smiled at Jeddal's furry back. The sun painted the topmost branches gold.

Throw it now, Father, Bog pleaded. Before the sun turned them both to stone.

In one swift motion, Jeddal gripped the boulder and rose to his full height, his roar echoing off the rocks in the clearing.

The thin man backed away—a scrawny wolf with flattened ears. Bog grinned. Finally, the man understood who was in charge.

"Turn on the music," the thin man yelled toward the puny one. "Now."

The puny one leapt from the hollow of ferns, gripping a flat, palm-sized box that glowed with silver light. With trembling fingers, he fiddled with the box.

Jeddal threw the boulder. Bog headed for the puny one, ready to knock him sideways, as a painful clamour burst from the box. A piercing noise ricocheted off the rocks and sliced into his ears.

"No!" He wound one arm over his head to protect his ears. With his other arm, Bog felt for loose rocks, boulders, bushes. He flung whatever he touched at the stabbing noise box.

"Stop!" he screamed.

The blare was endless. Bog's ears were ready to split open. Finally, it stopped as abruptly as it had begun. He uncovered his ears and shook his still-ringing head.

Jeddal must have been throwing, too. Rocks were strewn across the clearing, clumps of blueberries uprooted, prickly junipers scattered. A huge boulder cast a shadow over Bog, blocking his view of Jeddal. Sunlight beamed from the east, beyond the boulder, and his eyes burned as the world brightened.

The noise box was smashed. The humans had fled to the scrawny cedars about ten paces away—the thin man bleeding from his forehead. Bog smirked. Soon, they'd be running home, squealing.

The sun grew brighter, more dangerous. Even in the shadow of the boulder, Bog narrowed his eyes against its glare. He shadow-slipped backward, careful to avoid the sun's deadly rays. He peered around for Jeddal.

Jeddal wasn't there. Bog shadow-slipped forward.

The humans were advancing out of the trees, smiling, showing horrible flat teeth. Bog growled, stirring the air with his tail, yet they kept advancing. Why wasn't Jeddal howling at these humans?

Bog reached out to touch the boulder and then snatched his hand back in horror. He choked in a breath, gaping at the massive rock. Rounded ears, rugged cheeks, glorious warty nose. Jeddal? Lured into the sun and turned to stone?

"Father!" Bog wailed. How had the humans outwitted them?

A laugh rang out.

"The Troll Hunter was right. They are scared of music." It was the fat human's whining voice.

The vermin crept closer, fists raised.

"Where's your nest, troll?" The thin man smirked. "Where are the others?"

Bog growled. *Never hunt a human*, Jeddal had said. But they could hunt him and his family?

He crouched low and swung out with all his might, staying within Jeddal's shadow. He gripped the pulp of the fat man's forearm, dragged him into the shadows, and smacked a fist into the soft flesh of his gut. When the others ran at Bog, he tossed the fat man onto them. He punched and flailed until the humans fled into the sunlight, where Bog couldn't follow.

The thin man scurried to the centre of the clearing, his breath rasping and his nostrils flaring. The puny man tried to support the fat one, who was doubled over clutching his stomach.

"Cowards!" Bog yelled from the safety of Jeddal's shadow. "Finish the fight."

Silence hung between them. A finch and two cardinals dared to sing. A she-wolf called to her cubs.

The humans turned tail and ran south, darting between tiny patches of sun.

Bog roared until the forest was mute. Until only the rustle of the birches could be heard. Then he sank against the boulder that was now his father. He pressed his face against the cold stone. He let tears drip hopeful magic onto the rock.

The shadows shrank. The sun demanded its due. Bog collected the deer mice and followed Jeddal's shadow to the shade of the forest canopy.

His head hung heavy. His nose drooped. He headed home, doubling back repeatedly to mask his trail before hurrying through the shadows. Alone.

2

MOUSEMEAT STEW

EIGHT nights since Jeddal had been turned to stone.

The moonlight sliced through the swaying branches, making dappled patterns on the lichen-covered rocks. Bog searched every boulder for a nose or a twisted mouth, mourning the ancient stone trolls he'd always passed without ever thinking of the grieving families left behind.

Every step through their hunting grounds was a torment. He prodded the dead coals in the pothole where he and Jeddal had sometimes cooked a quick meal. He skirted the clearing where Jeddal's statue stood, replaying that horrible sunrise in his mind. If only they'd fought the humans after first catching their scent. If only he'd watched the puny man more closely.

Bog navigated the darkness, his chest aching. When he smelled a grouse hiding in the leaf litter, he remembered the youngsters' hungry bellies and Kasha's empty stewpot.

He slipped closer to the bird. Even in the shadows, it couldn't hide from him. He could see the crested head, although the bird's scent and pattering heart also gave it away. What a slow-witted bird. Impossible to miss.

Just like those humans should have been. First, their gas-snorting machines called cars invaded the forest. Then, their guns killed the big game. Now, their troll hunters destroyed families.

A gust of wind stirred the canopy of leaves. Bog edged toward the spot where the grouse hid without making a sound.

If only he could rid the world of troll hunters.

He stubbed his toe on a fist-sized rock that tumbled through last-season's leaves like a squirrel on a chase. The grouse burst upward, exploding through the undergrowth with a thunderous flapping of wings.

Bog lurched after it, stumbling over the rock he'd kicked. The grouse flew straight up, its tail fanned out. Bog snatched a fistful of tail feathers as it arched out of range.

His stomach twisted as if mangled by some vicious animal. He couldn't even get close to his prey. All he could do was hound the woods, brooding about Jeddal.

Enough. Although the sun was still hidden, he set his feet toward home. Maybe he could find some grubs along the way. His fists clenched and his tail dragged against the ferns.

As Bog neared the darkened entrance to the cave, Ruffan's furry head popped out.

"Get inside." Bog growled. "There may be troll hunters about."

Ruffan's eyes examined Bog's empty rucksack and fistful of grubs before he dove back into the tunnel, calling, "He's only brought crawlies again."

Bog hunched through the low tunnel, cursing. When he entered the fire-lit cave, he snarled at Ruffan, who tumbled away from the warning swat of Bog's hand and then rolled over Mica and Gem, who pushed him toward the fireplace.

"Yow!" Ruffan cried, holding his singed tail.

Then Mica pinched Gem, and she pinched him back.

Kasha whacked the three youngsters with a wooden spoon. Like any good grandmother, she ruled with a will of iron. She could also magic up trolls' gold out of a handful of coals, carve skis so they glided smoothly over the snow, and tell a story better than anyone Bog knew.

If only he'd brought her more than grubs.

With a sharpened fingernail, Kasha sliced the last of the mousemeat and threw it into the iron pot suspended over the fire. Her black eyes travelled to the pile of squirming wormlike creatures Bog deposited on the hearth.

"Wash for dinner, Bog." She turned back to the pot, the grey-white fur on her back standing on end.

Bog hung his head.

Ruffan, Mica, and Gem began to play a game on the floor, tossing stones into circle targets and negotiating trades. In a basin near the three tiny sleeping nooks, Bog tried to wash off the human stink that seemed to cling to his hide, even though he hadn't been close to a human in eight nights. By the time he finished, Kasha had set dinner out on the stone slab. Bog took his seat on a side bench, glancing at Jeddal's empty place at the head of the table.

For dinner, Kasha served mousemeat stew with mugs of watery broth to wash it down. Mica and Gem stuffed the stew into their mouths with both hands, but Ruffan was too delicate, holding his meat in two fingers and chewing with his mouth closed.

"Eat nicely, Ruffan," Kasha ordered, her white eyebrows like two stiff brushes.

Bog chewed steadily. The meat tasted bland. He finished his small helping before his stomach was full.

"I've heard talk." Kasha frowned at Bog. "Josaya was by."

His ears twitched. Their closest neighbour rarely ventured into their territory. "What did she want?"

"She said, 'Beware of a new human in the area. The Troll Hunter,'" continued Kasha. "He's stoning trolls everywhere."

The youngsters listened with wide eyes.

Bog scowled, slopping broth down his chin and then wiping it away with the back of his hand. "Those humans mentioned the Troll Hunter."

Kasha nodded. "He's set up a den where he teaches other humans how to trick us."

The broth in Bog's stomach rolled to a boil. Those humans had blasted the noise they called *music* at sunrise to distract them. Maybe they'd spoiled the hunt on purpose to force Jeddal and him to stay out longer. Was this trickery because of the Troll Hunter's teachings?

"The Troll Hunter's den is rumoured to be near Thunder City. He's training more hunters every day." Kasha's beady eyes were intense. "Within one moon, they'll be swarming our forest worse than ever. We need to move farther north, away from them."

"Again?" Bog ground his fist into his thigh. "Why do we have to run away with our tails dragging every time they get close? We should crush this Troll Hunter and his followers before they cause more damage. We should—"

Kasha slapped a hand on the stone slab, making the youngsters jump. "Did Jeddal teach you nothing? Stay away from humans."

"But they killed Jeddal!"

"Will killing humans bring him back? Will it feed the young-uns?" Kasha snorted. "Don't hoard your anger as if it's gold. It's not troll-like."

The stab of Kasha's glare silenced Bog, yet the idea of destroying the Troll Hunter and his followers was a vine spreading tendrils. He pushed his empty bowl away.

Wouldn't Jeddal have defended his family?

After dinner, Kasha got out her ointment pot, grabbed hold of Gem, and rubbed the acidic paste into the youngster's furry hide, stretching and pulling her nose. Because of Kasha, all the youngsters would grow a thick hide and long noses—she'd even improved Bog's stubby nose.

Bog's family was a mishmash of relations and orphans. Mica and Gem were twins whose parents had been crushed by a human's car, and Ruffan's mother had died at his birth. Jeddal was Kasha's son, and Bog was his, although Bog had no mother that he knew of. Jeddal would never talk about her, even when Bog pleaded for a story.

Kasha let Gem go, wiped the rest of the ointment onto her own red nose, and grabbed Mica for his treatment. "Make yourself useful, Bog." She gave him a challenging glare. "You can do the tally."

Bog trundled to the family treasure chest, opened the lid, and began to check their hoard. Even though the count rarely changed, Jeddal had tallied their treasure nightly, praising the sheen of the silver and the sparkle of the amethysts. Since Jeddal had been turned to stone, Bog had added nothing to their hoard and little to their stewpot. His tail quivered.

When Kasha finished with Mica and Ruffan, Bog was still working the tally. Kasha yanked her own nose a few more times, raked the coals, and settled on a stool beside the fire with a sigh. She'd worked twice as long on Ruffan to toughen his unusually smooth skin.

"Story time, story time," the youngsters chanted.

Mica and Ruffan toppled over each other to get to Kasha's feet, but Gem kicked them both out of the way.

Kasha let them settle and then asked, "Which story this morning?"

"The one about the sun!" Gem yelled. "How Grental captured the biggest ball of gold."

"No, we heard that one last morning." Mica scowled. "I want to hear about Troll Mountain, where the troll queen lives."

"Ymir and the first trolls who walked the land!" Ruffan squealed.

Kasha frowned, wrinkling her forehead. When she glanced at Bog, he bent over his work. He tried to keep the count, but silver didn't seem important this morning. All the lessons that Jeddal had yet to teach him—lost. All the hunts they could have shared—gone. Bog found his hands clenched.

"Leave that," Kasha said to Bog, her voice raspy. "I have a story for you."

"For me?" Bog's eyebrows arched.

"Why him? Not fair!" Gem yelled.

Kasha walloped each youngster with the back of her hand. "Tonight is Bog's turn. Now, off to sleep with you."

While Kasha corralled the youngsters into their sleeping nooks, Bog stacked the silver and amethysts and shut the chest. Maybe Kasha's story would be about the Troll Hunter or Jeddal. Either way, he knew to pay attention or risk a swatting.

Kasha crooned a few songs to settle the youngsters and then joined Bog by the fire. Together, they stared at the glowing, black-hearted coals, until the rustling and whispers of the youngsters faded. How many times had Bog listened to Kasha and Jeddal's fireside murmurs from the sleeping nook he shared with Ruffan? Now, he'd taken Jeddal's place.

"We trolls have a long history," Kasha finally began, "but each one of us has a tale, too. This tale is for you, Bog." Kasha's mouth was grim. "I saved the telling until the time was right."

Bog nodded, trying to keep focused on Kasha's story. Tendrils of smoke disappeared up the flue.

"Here's how it goes." Kasha voice was solemn. "As a young troll, Jeddal set out from home one evening.

He'd been hunting on his own for some time since his father, my mate, had been killed by humans near the village of Strongarm." Kasha's black eyes were fierce.

A familiar squeeze tightened Bog's chest. Tomorrow night he'd hunt the humans who tricked Jeddal. He could pick up their trail at Jeddal's statue—maybe it would even lead to the Troll Hunter's den. It couldn't be wrong to protect his family.

"Jeddal melted through the bushes, so quiet a hunter was he. He slid through pine and poplar like a worm through the earth, undetected by even the owl's keen eyes. That night, he found himself gliding parallel to a humans' road through our forests. The humans were using the road to trade between Strongarm and Thunder City, down in the south. Rutted and pitted was this road, with branches overhanging. Yet the poor state of the road gave Jeddal an idea. He would drag a log across it, forcing the humans' metal machines to stop. Soon, the humans would abandon the road, leaving us trolls in peace."

"I hope he blocked the humans," Bog muttered. He wanted a tale of sweet justice or no story at all.

Kasha nodded. "He didn't even need to find a log. That old road had done his work for him. You see, Jeddal found an overturned metal machine called a truck," she continued. "He could smell it first—three humans and poisonous gasoline on the forest floor.

The truck was boxy and large, the back filled with useless vegetables."

Bog scowled. Only Ymir knew why humans wanted to eat vegetables.

"When he got closer, he saw that a gaping hole in the road had tipped the truck, tossing two human men onto the nearby rocks, killing them. But Jeddal could hear the third human moving. So he jumped over, clearing the truck easily, to where he could hear the groaning of that last horrible human."

"Jeddal always was a good jumper," Bog said. He'd been good at most everything.

"The last human was a female. And this is what I know of her: She was pretty, not like most humans. She had a bumpy nose, coarse skin, and dark hair as wild as the wind. Her teeth were nicely gapped, although flat. Jeddal told me later that she could laugh like the tinkling of gold coins and skin a hare faster than he could. Yes, those two got to liking each other—a troll and a human, if you can believe it. After they got through the first few moments."

Jeddal—friendly with a human? Bog couldn't imagine it.

"Because what Jeddal saw when he swooped over was this bedazzling human female, a jewel herself, lifting the truck off her own legs, which were pinned underneath."

Bog snorted at Kasha's exaggeration. No human was that strong.

"And Jeddal was so startled to see a human with more strength than a fly that he stared. *Maybe she's a troll*, he thought, although it turned out that she was human, through and through.

"One thing I'm sure you learned from Jeddal," Kasha waggled a finger at him, "is to use the advantage of surprise. He always taught that one first, since he messed up on it this terrible time. While Jeddal stood with his mouth agape, the human female took charge. She rolled out from under that truck, grabbed a metal bar that had come loose, and knocked his legs out from under him."

More exaggeration. As if Kasha wanted him to be impressed by this human.

"Well, imagine Jeddal's surprise to find himself on the ground because of a human," Kasha continued. "He scrambled to his feet, awkward and clumsy, and found this human female on her feet, too. She was standing tall with a gun at her shoulder, propping herself against the side of the truck on two broken legs."

Impossible.

"Now, Jeddal couldn't believe a human had bested him," Kasha continued. "He was so amazed that he laughed outright, while that female was aiming a fool gun at him. Jeddal laughed until the tears wet his fur, and that human stared back at him, pointing the gun, until she began to laugh, too.

"That's the story of how Jeddal met a human.

Martinique Bottom, her name was. And those two became close, quite close. In fact, Martinique Bottom was," Kasha shot him a piercing look, "your mother."

"No!" Bog stood, roaring.

Half breed? Half a troll? It wasn't true. Jeddal, greatest of trolls, was his father. His nose was long and bent. His ears floppy. His treasure chest full.

But Kasha's steady eyes told him that she spoke the truth.

"That's why you're smaller, your tail so short and your nose blunt," Kasha said. "Your mother was a human."

"She couldn't be!" Bog smashed a fist into the cave wall. A trickle of pebbles fell from the spot.

That's when he noticed the youngsters, their heads poking through the archway into the common room, Ruffan's hand over his mouth, the twins silent and gaping. Bog turned from them, hating their eyes on him.

"Back to your burrows," Kasha ordered.

The youngsters scurried out of sight.

Kasha shook her head. "With all your anger at the hunters, I had to tell you, Bog. Each of us is upset about Jeddal, but you're ready to hunt humans instead of staying where you belong. That much rage—it's not natural for a troll. It's the human in you coming out."

He held his head in both hands to stop the cave walls from spinning.

"Your father couldn't stand your mother's rages—vicious as a weasel when she didn't get her way. He said they fought over where to live, how to raise you—everything. Still, he lived near Strongarm with that human for more than two summers. Until she did the unspeakable."

"What did she do?" How horrible could his mother be? And what did that make him?

Kasha shrugged. "Jeddal would never say. I only know that he took you away to shield you. So you wouldn't become like her."

Bog moaned, his head still swimming. How could Kasha even accept him—a half-human?

"Don't go chasing after the Troll Hunter or his followers," Kasha pleaded. "It'll only end badly. Learn from Jeddal's mistakes."

"I have to protect the family, even if it means killing the Troll Hunter." Bog tried to still the tremor that shook his whole body. He would track the humans who'd tricked Jeddal and find the Troll Hunter, too. And he'd destroy them all.

Kasha glared. "Honour Jeddal's wishes and stay away from humans. You don't want to become like them. Remember when Jeddal—"

"No more stories." Bog cut her off. Didn't she understand that it was because of Jeddal he had to go? He had to show that he was a worthy son, and now a worthy troll. "I'll leave when the sun sets."

3

THE FIRST STEP

THE next night, Bog stood with his back to the cave, his feet aimed south. Everyone had gathered to see him off. On his left, Kasha contemplated the forest, her mouth set in a stony grimace. On his right, Ruffan gripped Bog's hand, his whole body shivering. Mica and Gem were wrestling with each other beside Kasha's feet.

The cool, damp smell of the cave wafted from behind, along with the lingering scent of the broth and grubs they'd slurped for breakfast. Bog released Ruffan's hand, preparing to take the first step that would lead him away from home. Away from Kasha and the youngsters. Away from the places that brought back painful memories of Jeddal.

His feet wouldn't budge, although he knew he had to hurry. Every moment he hesitated meant that another troll hunter would be trained, and another family would suffer. But he had to make peace with Kasha first.

"Kasha, listen," Bog began, hoping she'd bless his leaving. "I've been a useless hunter anyway. And Ruffan's a good mouser and snaker. He needs to get out of the cave."

"Oh, yes." Ruffan leapt to Kasha's side. "Could I hunt, please? I caught a grouse once."

"Go, if you must, Bog," she rumbled low in her throat, ignoring Ruffan. "Just don't expect me to like it."

A pain shot through Bog's upper body, as if a slash of sunlight had cut across his flesh. Kasha didn't understand. He wasn't abandoning his family; he was proving he was worthy of them.

The sun had just set behind the trees, leaving a red-orange scar fading in the western sky. The eastern sky was clouding over. Only a patch of stars flashed like fireflies between the swaying branches.

A muddy footprint marked the stone before his feet. As large as Kasha's stewpot, the footprint must be one of Jeddal's. Soon the rain would wash it clear and fall like tears over the stone statue of Jeddal.

Bog resettled his rucksack on his shoulder and cast another glance at Kasha. When he saw the hard edge to her mouth, he pulled his feet free of the roots that bound them.

"I'll be off now." Bog nodded to Ruffan. "Hunt well."

"You, too." Ruffan wiped a hand across his watery eyes.

Mica and Gem became strangely motionless. Gem had a beefy arm wrapped around Mica's neck and Mica had a hold of Gem's ear—a solemn pause in their fight, in his honour.

"I've one bit of magic for you." Kasha stepped forward. She shoved Jeddal's flint stone into his rucksack to join his jug of mousemeat stew and jug of broth.

It was magic, of a sort. Like carrying Jeddal with him. "Thanks." He tugged Kasha's nose affectionately.

"We'll be heading farther north," she said, "to the lakeside cave where we camped two summers ago. If it's occupied, we'll be nearby. Do you remember the way?"

He nodded, wishing they didn't need to flee.

"Be cunning, Bog." A cloud of flies whirled above her head. She yanked his nose to say goodbye.

"I will." He rubbed noses with the youngsters and then clumped over the rippled stone and into the bush. Behind him, Mica and Gem grunted as they resumed their wrestling match.

"Come home to us." Bog heard Kasha's whisper even with the growing distance between them.

He didn't look back.

The forest coated the land like a rumpled blanket over the bones of an old troll. Bog travelled by scent through the darkest undergrowth and then tromped over the rocky ground of the clearing toward Jeddal.

A half-formed snarl remained trapped on Jeddal's lips. His motionless eyes unnerved Bog. He touched Jeddal's stone nose. It was cold. Unyielding.

Bog's fingernails dug into his palms. His eyes brimmed with tears.

"Goodbye, Father." He rubbed his eyes to clear them and silently vowed to make Jeddal proud. Then he inhaled deeply, alert for the humans' scent trail.

He picked it up near the south edge of the clearing. It was fading, but still strong enough to point the way. After a final glance at Jeddal, Bog plunged into the forest, following the foul humans who'd lured Jeddal into the sun.

Their trail meandered between rocky mounds and then ran parallel to a narrow stream. When it circled the crumple of wood that was his great-grandfather Mithanen, Bog had no time for a visit. When Mithanen had been alive, the old troll had bounced Bog so hard on his knee that he'd launched Bog into the air, shrieking and laughing. Unlike Mithanen, Jeddal wouldn't have the honour of old age, with moss sprouting from his fleshy ears. He wouldn't shrink and warp until the night he became so ancient that he'd walk into the forest to twist into a sculpture of boughs, limbs, and twigs. Jeddal had been turned to rock before his life was even half over.

Bog ploughed into less familiar territory. He lost the trail once, but picked it up again after circling the area twice. When he detected the mouldy odour of a couple of wood spirits, he gave them a wide berth to avoid the lure of their siren-like call. *You only hear a wood spirit's call once*, Jeddal had said. Too many trolls had been turned to forest rot—fuel for the wood spirit's trees.

In the distance, a wood owl hooted. Frogs called from the nearby pond. The scents of chipmunks mapped their recent trails. Bog smelled no trolls nearby, which suited him fine. He'd rather sleep in a hole during a hurricane than stumble into another cave troll's home for a violent welcome. Even worse than cave trolls, he'd heard that western mountain trolls grew larger and meaner. And northern trolls, who could have up to twelve heads, were tough enough to survive shortened nights in the summer.

The scent trail continued south into human territory. It probably ended at Strongarm—the closest town. He vaguely knew the way, although he'd never been.

Jeddal had, of course, with Martinique Bottom.

Bile rose in his throat. Oh, Ymir, how had Jeddal tolerated a human? How had he tolerated Bog? It was a mockery. Jeddal turned to stone by humans while his own son was half human.

Bog's hands became fists. He wanted to smash the biggest boulder he could find into a mountainside.

He wanted to rip the tallest tree out of the ground and hurl it across the ocean. He wanted to—

He stopped, his feet on the edge of a dirt road made by humans. The stench of oil filled his nostrils. He wanted to retch. Was he so stunned that he forgot to pay attention to where he was going? Could he not smell oil before he stepped on it?

Bog stood, transfixed. Maybe he was as dumb as a human. And as weak as one.

He sniffed around for the humans' trail.

Gone.

He flicked his tail back and forth. Maybe they'd travelled away in one of their metal machines.

Bog scowled, scanning both ways down the road. He heard no machines. Just the buzz of insects and the scurry of rodents. His quest couldn't end here— at the side of a humans' road through a trolls' forest. He paced parallel to the road, clenching his jaw.

A trap. He would set a trap for the fool humans. Just like Jeddal would have done. Maybe it would deceive those troll hunters the next time they ventured by. He glanced at the still-dark sky; he had time before he needed to find a cave or a hole in the ground.

Bog tossed a raccoon-sized rock onto the middle of the road. He smacked it, saying *fnorb*, the word "rock" backward in troll talk. His hand tingled with the magic. The rock shimmered. The surface of it rippled like water and then the rock gradually faded—invisible, until a human's machine smacked into it. It was a simple shape-shimmer trick, but it would make trouble for the humans.

He continued along the road travelling south—he wasn't sure where else to go. Maybe he could find Thunder City, where the Troll Hunter's den was rumoured to be.

When he could, he ripped out the signs covered in the human's squiggly markings and left them on the road. He shape-shimmered more rocks. He stomped potholes into the road. Jeddal would have been pleased, but Bog wished he could do more.

Where the road tunnelled through a rocky hill, Bog dragged a bear-sized boulder in front of the tunnel entrance. He was about to shape-shimmer the boulder when he heard a voice, coming from the tunnel.

"Hello, friend." It spoke in a troll dialect, but with a twangy accent. The tunnel took the voice and bounced it off the walls, making it boom.

Bog tensed as the biggest forest troll he'd ever seen emerged from the tunnel. The troll looked like an enormous shaggy bear, even bigger than Jeddal.

"I'm Small." The troll stopped in front of the boulder, each thigh as thick as Bog's waist. He smelled like fresh leaves, and his nose was admirably long. "Who are you?"

"You're hardly small." Bog's mouth was dry, his palms sweaty.

The troll grinned. He didn't seem threatening.

Then Bog heard the faint hum of a human's

machine echoing through the tunnel. Two bright lights behind the troll threw his massive shadow over Bog and the boulder. A cold sweat broke over his body.

"Watch out!" Bog growled. He didn't know if a metal machine could flatten this huge troll, but he didn't want to find out.

The troll spun around to face the machine, losing his balance. As he fell, he whacked his head against the boulder and then slid to the ground.

The machine roared into the tunnel. The troll was out cold. Bog grabbed him under his furry armpits and heaved as hard as he could.

The troll didn't budge.

"Come on." Bog's shoulders tightened. His blood raced.

A boxy machine—it had to be a truck—bore down on them, roaring and screaming, lights blinding. Bog tugged with all his strength, dragging the troll onto the loose gravel of the road's edge just as the stinking truck shot out of the tunnel. As it approached, it suddenly jerked to one side and swerved around the boulder, slowing briefly before it zoomed out of sight.

Bog shook his fist after the truck, coughing and cursing in a cloud of dust and foul-smelling smoke.

4

SMALL

SMALL rubbed the back of his head. "I don't get how you did it, Bog, but I'm sure glad you saved me."

"And I don't get how you recovered so quickly." Bog stood awkwardly at the edge of the road, unsure of how to deal with this unusually friendly troll.

"It takes a lot to bring me down." Small shrugged. "Although I could use a rest after that blow. Come on."

He tromped several paces into the dense forest of spruce and sank onto an old log. After a moment, Bog followed. Fragrant needles cushioned his feet, and resin-scented branches brushed his arms.

"I'm surprised you could even lift me. You're undersized for a cave troll," Small said as Bog sat next to him. "No fur on your face either. Why, you could even pass for a human." He guffawed, walloping Bog hard on the shoulder.

Bog's tail curled. Small's words pricked like a knife at a wound. If only Small knew. Then he wouldn't be so friendly.

"You'd make a perfect human." Small flicked his long bushy tail toward Bog's shorter one. "We could dress you in a pair of trousers, a shirt, and some boots, tuck in your tail, and send you off to town to pick up the mail." Small laughed, snorting in the long, tawny fur that grew around his mouth and everywhere else—so different from Bog's bristled grey fur.

"What is *mail*?" Bog asked, silently vowing that he'd never play-act as a human.

Small's furry eyebrows rose. "Don't you know? Humans write notes to one another. They consider it valuable stuff. If you take their mail, they give you food to get it back."

"How do you know so much about humans?" Bog frowned. Could Small somehow sense that he had human blood?

"I live in a forest-troll settlement near Strongarm, so we tangle with them all the time. Humans are a stupid lot. You can get away with anything."

"Near Strongarm? I'm heading south—toward Thunder City."

"That right? Why don't you stay with us on your way through? It's the least I can do since you saved me from that truck." Small cleared the fur from his eyes.

"Really?" Would the other forest trolls be as huge as Small? As friendly? Maybe Bog could learn from them—about humans and how to conquer them. Maybe they'd know more about the Troll Hunter.

"Sure thing. Anything I can do for you, Bog, just let me know. I owe you a *gnark*—a life debt," Small said solemnly. "And I'll repay the favour, if I can."

For the first time in many nights, Bog managed to smile.

"Well, there's one thing you could do…" Bog began.

"Yeah?"

"What do you know about the Troll Hunter?"

Small frowned. "We've heard plenty about him, and it's all bad. You're not going after him—a little troll like you?"

Bog shrugged, not wanting to admit his plan. "I hear he's set up a den near Thunder City, so I should be prepared."

"Well, I can tell you what I know, and we can hear the latest news back in my settlement. But first, I've got a job to do tomorrow night." Small nodded toward the northeast. "You could help me with it, and then we could head south together. Do you want to rid the world of a logging camp?"

Bog had never seen a logging camp, but Jeddal had told him how loggers destroyed the forests, tree by tree.

"I guess." He could scare some humans away from the forest, and his family, while he learned about the Troll Hunter.

Small grinned. "Great. I've got a hollow tree nearby that I snug up in sometimes. It should fit two if we carve out the earth. And, I happen to make a flavoursome travellers' stew. I've got all the ingredients here." He hefted his rucksack, which was twice the size of Bog's.

Bog's stomach gurgled at the mention of food.

"Sounds like your stomach is interested," Small said.

"Thanks." Bog sniffed in the direction of Small's rucksack, taking in the delicious scent of meat—hare probably. He thought of the weak mousemeat stew he'd brought. He could share it with Small, if he wanted any.

They began walking northeast. Bog hurried to keep pace with Small, who took one step for every two of his. The darkness was a cool comfort, although soon a faint blush would lighten the eastern sky.

"Now," Bog began, "tell me about the Troll Hunter."

Over the next day and night, Bog heard stories about the Troll Hunter—about how this fanatical human had recently arrived from the western lands, where he'd been waging war on the fierce mountain trolls;

how he'd built a campaign against nearby trolls by training other humans to destroy them; and how he'd been tracked to Thunder City in the south, although no troll had gotten close enough to be sure it was him without coming to harm.

With every moment, Bog became more determined to stop him.

Bog learned more about humans, too. How they hoarded boxes of meat in huge buildings called stores. How they valued rectangular paper called money as much as they did gold. How they used machines for everything from travelling to cooking to talking to one another across vast distances. And how their logging camp was fouling Small's settlement.

"The logging camp sends sludge down the river, killing the fish. Pa said to me, 'I've got a small job for you.' You see, I'm the biggest, so when they've got a huge job they call it a small job. Get it?" Small chuckled. "I always get sent to the logging camp."

"You do this often?"

"Once in a while, usually in the spring. I knock it down, and they build it up again. This time, I want to figure out a way to make them leave for good." Small quickened his pace. "Come on, I'll show you where the forest ends. That's a sight you won't believe."

The trees grew as thick as ever, with tall straight trunks that stretched for the sky. Bog had seen how humans made a space among the trees to build a cabin. Would the forest end in a clearing at the logging camp?

They travelled northeast, away from Strongarm, crossing a narrow dirt road that stank of gas. The forest closed around them again, the branches so tight they had to walk single file. From behind Small, Bog caught the whiff of oil up ahead, and a breeze from an open space. The scent of humans was strong—that sour, fatty odour that wafted off them, so like the stench of their garbage.

Then Small stepped into a mud-covered clearing lit by a starry sky. Bog gaped at the sight. Vast tracts of mucky hills, the trees ripped from the earth, only stumps left and scattered twigs. Hill after hill of harsh wasteland, as far as he could see. Bog clenched his jaw.

"Not a good place to travel," Small sighed so hard his shoulders shuddered. "No cover. But I wanted you to see this."

They trudged silently along the edge of the forest. Bog kept snatching glances at the barren hills. No trees, just a few scrubby bushes with roots latching feebly onto earth and rock. Stumps everywhere. Broken branches. Limbs snapped in two. He could understand taking a few trees to build, or eat, or whatever they did with them. But why so many at once? How would the forest grow again? Where would the trolls live? The animals?

The river, when he came to it, was thick sludge, littered with leaves and debris. A putrid smell of mould and death wafted from it. Bog turned away, nose stinging.

"When they take the trees," Small began, "the muck gets washed into the river. Leaves and branches, too. And sawdust, bark, garbage. All of it gets swept down to us. Suffocates the fish."

Bog's head spun from the stench.

Across the river, the forest was blissfully untouched.

"We'll cross here," Small said. "Travel upriver in the shadows."

Bog hated to put even a toe in the water, but he followed Small's lead. The river-bottom was oozing, soft, and fleshy. The chill water came up to Bog's chest and stink invaded his fur. Back on land, he tried to shake off the sludge, but a thin coating clung. He shivered in the light breeze.

From the lush south bank, they tramped upriver. The loggers' destruction continued on the opposite bank, like a naked bleeding sore. They walked until their fur dried. The destruction ended as abruptly as it had begun. Soon, the stench cleared.

Upriver, the water shimmered in the starlight, free from sludge. The river was smooth, dotted with the reflections of the stars. Two bats whizzed past, shady hunters zooming low over the water for mosquitoes.

They crossed back to the north side of the river. Bog dunked and scrubbed his fur to clear the lingering stench and then rolled in sweet-smelling leaves.

"The camp's not far," Small whispered. He shook to dry himself.

They smelled the camp before they saw it—more reek of human sweat. From the bushes, they saw a low wooden building lit by a single bulb over the door and eight rough canvas tents. Two men with bare chests lounged outside one of the tents. Their flesh was smooth, almost hairless. No wonder they usually covered it with cloth. They were smoking cigarettes, Small explained, and drinking from metal cans. Felled trees and sawdust surrounded the camp.

"It's bigger than before." Small grunted. "Every time, it's a bit worse."

"We've got to close them down." Bog wanted to lunge at those humans, but that wouldn't stop them from bringing more loggers. Shape-shimmer tricks wouldn't be enough either. Nor would smashing down the building. What would Jeddal have done?

With Bog's belly complaining and legs aching, he couldn't come up with an answer. "We should kill them all," he muttered. "Every last one of them."

Small shook his head. "That's what humans would do."

Bog flinched.

"But it wouldn't work," Small continued. "It never ends." He sighed. "I've got a hole nearby—if it hasn't been flattened. We can work out a plan there."

Back in the forest, Bog started a fire with Jeddal's flint stone. He tried to think of a way to stop the loggers, but he couldn't wipe the fields of destruction from his mind. Tree carcasses everywhere. Humans were vile beasts. How could he be one of them? He almost felt responsible. As if he'd been fool enough to cut down the trees himself. He grimaced. He had to put a stop to it, somehow.

They devoured another of Small's fine stews and brooded by the fire. Bog stared at the flames, rubbing the flint stone between his thumb and finger. Jeddal had preferred to trick humans, not kill them. Was that because he hadn't wanted Bog to injure his own kind?

When Small began to yawn, they squished into a tight hole. Small fell asleep as the birds began chirping, but Bog squirmed, trying not to disturb him. His eyelids were heavy, but his mind raced. Could he do nothing to stop these humans? He reached into his rucksack and fumbled for Jeddal's stone. If only it could spark an idea.

Just as Bog was drifting into sleep, he heard a sorrowful moan in the distance. It was a song of longing. A sweet lament given with waning breath. It tugged at him, making him want to follow it, to live within it for eternity. Soon, others took up the cry, until the rocks echoed their call.

Bog couldn't resist. He dropped Jeddal's stone and squeezed past Small, who had rolled onto his side with a furry arm draped over his ear. As Bog emerged from the den, a wood spirit drifted between nearby bushes and branches, a translucent blur among the shadowy trees. Bog inhaled her enchanting scent of musty wood. As her song trembled from her throat, a craving for the pulp of forest rot strengthened within him. If only he could roll in it, bury himself in it forever. He didn't care that the sun was about to rise.

She glided away, following the distant calls of her sisters. Bog stumbled after her, colliding with a pine tree, knocking his head against a branch.

What was he doing? He glanced around. Wood spirits?

He should wake Small. They needed to flee...or hide...

As the wood spirits wandered farther away, their hold on Bog lessened. They were weakened by the loss of their trees. Otherwise, he'd never have broken free of their deadly cries.

Yet, if Bog could talk to them, work with them... maybe the wood spirits could haunt the logging camp. As long as Bog and Small could resist them. Bog remembered that Jeddal used to put pine gum in his ears to block their call.

The song of the wood spirits faded in the distance. Bog crawled back into the den and curled into a ball, the damp earth cool against his cheek. Beside him, Small's snores shook crumbs of soil from the roof of their hole. Bog's fingers found Jeddal's flint stone. He smiled in the darkness. Tomorrow night, he'd talk to the wood spirits.

5

WOOD SPIRITS

HALFWAY to sunrise, shadows clustered under the trees. Faint stars brightened the gaps between branches. The mouldy scent of wood spirits drifted toward the thicket north of the logging camp, where Bog and Small crouched, waiting.

"I guess you've got to be crafty because you're so tiny, Bog," Small said for the third time, "but do you figure we can trust them?"

Bog ignored the insult, even though it irked him. "They said they would help." If the wood spirits cooperated, it could be glorious. He could get rid of the loggers and scare away any other humans from the forests.

Earlier that night, Bog had approached a wood spirit who called herself Sateen. Even though the wood spirits had tormented the humans each time they returned to the area, it hadn't been enough. The roar of the machines blocked their siren-like call, and the wood spirits didn't have the strength to leave the forest and enter the clearing where the loggers made their camp. But now, with any luck, wood spirits and trolls would banish these humans together.

Darkness enveloped the logging camp, with only one brilliant light burning above the door to the building. They could hear loud snores from the tents, and a few mutterings. Bog inhaled the scents of the forest—the dung of white-tailed deer, dry dust of rock, wet earth, birch, and cedar—letting the odours churn and blend into a powerful fragrance.

When he noticed Sateen wafting in the distance, he rose, muscles tensed. He didn't risk a glance at Small, although he could sense him standing, too, the fur on his forearm brushing Bog's.

Sateen was translucent with twiggy limbs and brown bark-like skin. Her face and long hair were pale green and glowing softly. She and the other wood spirits glided through and around the tree trunks, sighing laments. When one collapsed, unable to float any farther, two others carried her off, moaning.

The effect of their song strengthened as they neared. Bog shuddered, reaching for his rucksack. He'd never seen a wood spirit turn a troll to rot, and he had no intention of experiencing it. He rummaged in his rucksack until he found the ball of pine gum that he'd wrapped in a leaf. As the scent of pine and rot mingled, he divided the sticky ball in half.

Small was leaning toward the wood spirits with an expression of deep desire on his face. Bog smacked him hard in the chest, until Small blinked and jerked back.

"Thanks, Bog." Small grunted, taking his share of the gum.

They plugged their ears, muting the wood spirits' call. As his head cleared, Bog breathed a sigh of relief. The aching hunger lessened.

They emerged from the thicket to greet Sateen, who flowed closer. Small stepped back, a scowl on his face.

Bog unplugged one ear, cautiously. The wood spirits had halted their call, for now, but Bog kept his pine gum handy, just in case.

"You know what to do?" He asked Sateen in his own language, knowing she'd understand. Wood spirits could ensnare in many languages.

She nodded, her hair flowing like a cluster of bracken fern. "We will suspend them in eternal longing." Her voice had a deep moaning quality.

Bog felt the too-familiar yearning again, as if a vast hole existed in his life that could only be filled if Sateen spoke more, longer.

He banged his ear to clear it.

Small let out a growl. He'd removed one earplug, too.

"Once I round them up, you can torment the humans however you want," Bog told Sateen. "Together, we'll make sure no humans ever return."

Sateen bobbed up and down, saying nothing.

"I'll set up the gold." Bog pushed through the undergrowth toward the clearing, removing his second earplug. He needed to be able to listen for humans.

Small followed.

"One troll is enough." Bog gestured for Small to stay put. "Besides, your size will scare them."

Small glanced apprehensively at the wood spirits who were forming a semi-circle around him. "I guess you're right." He fumbled with the pine gum, pushing it firmly into both ears.

Bog would have felt safer with his ears plugged, and stronger with Small by his side. But he needed to slip into the camp and get the humans to follow his trail to the wood spirits' trap. And what better way to lure humans than with trolls' gold? If only he could conjure it without trouble.

Bog skulked soundlessly into the logging camp. He hated being out in the open, exposed under the wide sky. He crept between two tents, avoiding the pegged ropes and the circle of light cast by the single bulb over the door to the low wooden building. To one side of the building was a stone-rimmed firepit. Bog rummaged in the cold bed of coals, gathering any large chunks. Some he added to a sack he'd fashioned from birch bark and slung on a reed rope around his waist. Others he piled in a pyramid on the wooden table near the firepit. Then, with a sharp rap, he whacked the pile.

"*Flachner groor ibem tor*," he chanted, saying the charm that would turn the coal to false-gold—he hoped. He'd done it often enough with Kasha looking on.

With a small whooshing sound, the coal began to brighten, glowing at first from within and then slowly seeping outward to transform each lump into shining gold.

Bog smiled, pleased he'd done it on his first try.

Trolls' gold gleamed brighter than real gold, although it should fool the humans. After a while, it would return to its original form. By then, he prayed to Ymir, the humans would be trapped by the wood spirits.

He worked his magic on the coals in his sack next. Then he tore a hole in the bottom of the sack with his fingernails so that smaller gold pieces would fall out, leaving a trail.

When he was finished, the trolls' gold glimmered on the table like a tiny false sun. And when he shook his sack, pebbles of gold fell through the hole onto the ground.

He was ready.

The sky was dark indigo, the sun still far from rising. Bog took a deep breath and then called out in the human tongue, thankful Jeddal had made him learn it. "Help! Troll in the camp!"

He thumped around the clearing, weaving between the tents. Noise erupted from the closest tent.

"Wake up, Vince," called a male voice. "Troll in the camp."

A heavy thud sounded, and then Vince, presumably, began to swear. "What do you think you're doing, Joe?"

"Stop bellyaching and get up!" said the first man—Joe. "There's a troll outside."

Tents became illuminated from inside. Sounds bombarded from all directions. Bog could hear the swish of a blanket tossed and the rustle of cloth.

His heart pounded along with the boots coming to get him. He had to stay ahead of them. Although Small could free him if he got caught, Bog prayed to Ymir that his plan would work.

He huddled near the wooden table where his bait lay shimmering. "Come get me," he whispered.

Shadowy figures appeared. Bog wanted to run, although he forced himself to linger. Better to wait until he'd baited them all.

He hunched over the gold, as if protecting it. They hadn't heard him rummaging around their firepit, and they wouldn't smell him either. The useless humans would have to rely on sight. It would take them ages to find him under the night's cloak.

Bog counted twelve humans so far. They were using flashlights to aid their eyes. Any moment, one would spot him, and the race would begin.

His muscles quivered, ready for flight. He had to trap as many as possible to make his plan work.

"Can you see anything, Vince?"

The ones called Joe and Vince were out now—the first to wake and last to emerge. Bog listened to his quarry, peering into the darkness. One human had even come out from the building. About twenty in all.

"Can't see no troll," said Vince.

Vince was a gangly man with lazy movements. Beside him, Joe was a runt with a disgustingly strong odour.

Ignoring the stench, Bog took a long breath and snarled, deep and throaty. It filled the logging camp—between the tents, under the scattered tables—and rumbled out to the rim of trees.

"What was that?" said a new voice.

"This is some joke," Vince yelled. "Get away with you, whoever you are."

"Sounds real to me, Vince." Joe's voice had a tremble in it. He hung behind Vince's skinny frame. "Too bad the Troll Hunter ain't here."

Yes, it was. Because then Bog could ensnare him, too. Bog filled his lungs and snarled again, louder this time. He shifted his arms so the gleam of the gold escaped. When a flashlight pinned him in its beam, he squinted.

"There! I see him."

"He's got gold!"

"Gold?"

"Let me at him."

Their lights burned. Bog slumped one shoulder, painted on his stupid mask, and glanced around sluggishly, as if just realizing others were near.

"Don't be a fool! He's dangerous."

"Naw, he's just a small one."

"Surround him! Get the gold."

"It ain't real. Only silver around here."

"Sure looks real!"

Several more flashlights locked Bog in their glare. He could only peer through his lashes; his eyes were sharp with pain. The lights crisscrossed around, above, on him. He was eager to flee the closing net.

The humans drew nearer. Bog slackened his jaw, let out one last snarl, scooped up as much gold as he could carry, and began a loping run toward the woods.

"He's taking the gold!"

His back was exposed, his body tight, waiting for the impact of some kind of weapon. He hoped a gunshot couldn't puncture his half-human hide. He ran, fueled by fear and exhilaration. He could still hear the humans arguing about whether to gather the remaining gold or go for him. With one elbow, he bumped his sack, still strapped to his waist, so that some gold pebbles fell in a trail behind him.

"He's dropping more."

"Let's get him!"

Bog pushed into the dark forest like a rock plunging into water, drawing them after him just as he'd planned. Bushes tugged at his fur. Branches scraped his arms. He crashed through everything in his path, his fur clumping with sweat, his eyes still aching.

Bog ran madly, fiercely, through the trees toward the hollow that Sateen had chosen. He hoped all the humans were following, but he didn't look. He wasn't going back for anything.

He passed through the hollow without stopping, hardly daring to glance at the floating wood spirits who were ready to trap the humans. His breath came in gasps. He struggled for air. When he was far enough away from the hollow, he collapsed beside a log. Only then did he realize how daring he'd been—partnering with wood spirits and surrounding himself with humans when only three had outsmarted Jeddal.

He grasped his sides, breathing fast and shallow. Whenever they'd encountered humans on their hunts, Jeddal had always sheltered Bog with his body, even hiding him in the undergrowth as a youngster. Now, Bog wondered if Jeddal had thought him too weak to do much good. He wished Jeddal could see him now.

When he caught the scent of Small, coming toward him, Bog managed a smile.

"I hope the wood spirits get them," Bog said, still breathing heavily.

Small sat on the log beside him. He nodded nervously. They secured the pine gum in their ears and waited. Would the wood spirits do their part?

Bog could smell humans and forest rot, wood spirits and gasoline. After ages of wondering, weakened without his sense of hearing, he and Small circled back to the hollow, leaving the mostly empty sack of trolls' gold behind. Had his plan worked?

The mouldy scent grew stronger as they approached, a cross between sugary sap and rotten wood. The bodies were encased in a large, glowing, greenish fog—humans floating horizontally in the dip in the forest, gently nudging branches, gripped in deceivingly peaceful poses.

"It worked," he called loudly to Small without removing his earplugs.

Small shivered. "It's not natural," he bellowed back.

Bog nodded.

They stepped between the suspended bodies, avoiding touching them. When Bog brushed against one accidentally, he felt the fog invade like slivers, stabbing and freezing. He jerked his arm away.

"Where's Sateen?" he yelled. He wanted to know if all the humans had been caught, and then he wanted to escape.

Small shrugged and glanced around. "Let's get away from here."

Bog held up a hand. "After we finish with Sateen," he shouted.

Small opened his mouth to reply as Sateen drifted

through the crowd of suspended bodies. Bog warily removed one earplug when she began to speak in troll talk.

"I kept my part of the bargain. You promise me that no humans will come here again?" Sateen's pale green face glowed the same colour as the fog around the humans. Bog could see through her to the bodies and branches behind. He felt the pull of her voice and stepped back.

"Do what I say and none will return." He made his voice sound confident, even though he wasn't. "Release one human tomorrow night. Make sure he's well enough to return home to tell the tale. Then let loose another the next night. Three at the most— you can keep the rest."

"I still don't understand why we should release any."

"They'll warn others not to come here." Bog hoped the horror of the wood spirits would scare away any more humans—keep them out of the forest and away from his family.

Sateen nodded. "A wise plan. I will release two humans, once we're done with them."

"Don't wait too—" Bog began.

But Sateen was leaning into the nearest body, pushing her face full into the fog. It was the man called Vince. His eyes were half-closed in a dull trance. He had one arm under his head as a pillow, and his legs were entwined. When Sateen began to exhale, more green fog gusted from her mouth and enveloped him. His eyes widened and an expression of terror gripped his face. As the fog whirlpooled around him, the mouldy scent grew even more powerful.

Bog could hardly watch as Vince's skin slowly darkened and thickened into rotting wood. He felt dizzy. Sickened. This wasn't the glorious moment of triumph he'd expected.

Maybe even humans deserved better than this.

Small tugged his arm. "Let's go."

Plugging his ear, Bog backed away with Small, careful to avoid touching any bodies. They needed distance between them and the wood spirits before they found a place to rest for the day. Then Bog needed to destroy the Troll Hunter.

6

THE BODY OF YMIR

"**H**E'S a cave troll!"

"Why's he here?"

The forest trolls stared. Bog wanted to shrink into a hole in the ground. If they knew he was half human, they'd chase him away, for sure.

"This troll is a hero." Small's shout halted every troll within hearing distance. "Bog has saved us all."

Every eye was on Bog. Every nostril took in his scent. He tucked his tail against his leg for comfort and then flicked it away, embarrassed. It had taken a night and a half to reach Small's settlement, and it had rained most of the time. Now, the sky was cloudless, although the faces of these forest trolls were as unfriendly as a thunderstorm.

Small climbed onto a rock platform that jutted into an open space beneath giant evergreens.

Nearby trolls scrambled toward the rock. More forest trolls appeared as if from nowhere, until Bog noticed holes in the earthy hillsides carefully hidden by bushes or rocks. These forest trolls clustered their homes into a tight knot.

"Let me explain about this cave troll," Small yelled, and he launched into the story of how Bog had pulled Small from the path of a truck and then partnered with wood spirits to frighten the loggers from returning.

Bog sniffed the crowd uneasily. A troll mother, smelling of milk, carried a baby in a birch-bark basket on her back. A troll with the odour of dung pulled a large cow by a rope leash. These trolls had only one head each, and they were as furry as Small, although they were closer to Bog's height.

As Small shared his tale, the faces began to change. Bog found it hard to read their expressions beneath all that fur, but he sensed a shift. Maybe they wouldn't run him out of the settlement. Several trolls edged closer to the rock platform, not with fists raised, but with words of celebration.

"The loggers are gone!"

"Hurray for Small!"

As if Bog had nothing to do with it? He scowled, feeling unwelcome and foreign.

"No, it was Bog who—" Then Small was besieged.

They swarmed Small, whacking his shoulders, yanking his nose, stroking the fur on his back.

So many trolls. So many smells. Bog looked

around for a retreat from the gathering throng. Then he scented the human.

He growled, deep and low, scanning the crowd until he found its source. A girl child? In Small's settlement?

She was sitting on the knee of an elderly female troll and watching him. The girl was tiny, but old enough to cause damage. Bog's fingers curled into fists. Even if these forest trolls couldn't accept him, he could still rid them of a human.

He pushed through the trolls and strode toward her, snarling.

The girl cowered.

The elderly troll shielded the girl with her body. "Stay away!" Her eyes were stabbing thorns.

From behind Bog, strong hands snaked around his chest and pulled him back. He inhaled Small's scent.

"No, Bog!"

Bog ripped Small's arms off his chest and spun around. "She shouldn't be here. She'll only make trouble."

Small's eyes held a twinkle of amusement. "You don't understand. We keep her for trade," he said. "The fool humans trust us when we return their kin undamaged."

The words took a moment to sink in. Bog had heard that mountain trolls used to eat humans, but trade them? He frowned. These forest trolls had disturbing habits.

Small laughed. A few others joined in. Bog's ears grew hot.

"You have much to learn about how to deal with humans," Small said. "Come on. Meet my pa. Let us handle the girl."

Bog trailed Small, relieved to leave the crowd, although he couldn't resist a last glance at the girl, who was nuzzled into the troll for comfort. Had Martinique Bottom coddled him like that? He shuddered. Although Kasha would say that any youngster deserved proper care, Bog couldn't help but be repulsed by this girl.

Small ducked into an entrance to an underground cavern, large enough to fit even him. The room they entered was a common area with well-worn rocks to sit on and a wooden table and chairs at one end. Simple, like at home, but with an earthy smell. A few coals glowed in a stone hearth, barely lighting the room. Bog could smell the remains of a delicious stew—probably grouse—and his stomach growled. A tawny-grey lynx with tufted ears wove between the table legs. As Small lumbered toward the table, ducking his head to avoid dangling roots, the lynx leapt out and pounced on Small's foot.

Small's laughter echoed off the walls. He scooped up the lynx and rubbed under its chin. It purred against his chest.

"Sit down," Small said.

Bog sat, savouring the comfort of the curved stone, well-fitted to his back.

Small waved at a bulky lump of rags in a corner. "Meet my pa, Frantsum."

Bog inhaled a faint scent of troll, masked by the smell of stew. The corner was in shadows, but he gradually made out the wrinkled features of an ancient troll.

"Just the two of us now," Small said, "but we get along fine."

Small's father must be almost ready for his final walk in the forest. He already had the scent of wood about him.

"Greetings, Frantsum." Bog shifted uneasily, hoping he'd be accepted.

"Good nightfall, Bog. I heard your name shouted outside." Frantsum's voice crackled with age. "If my son is praising you from the rock ledge, you must be a hero worthy of a feast."

"Uh, thanks." A feast to honour him—now that was unexpected. "I'm hungry enough to eat a whole bear." Bog stifled a yawn. The noises from outside the cavern still bombarded him. So much had happened in the last few nights. Although Bog wished he could return to his own cave for a quiet night of stories, he was determined to carry on with his mission against the Troll Hunter.

"Our hero's tired," Frantsum croaked. "Small, find him a place to rest while we arrange the celebration. We'll show these trolls what a hero looks like."

The celebration turned out to be disturbingly huge, with more trolls together than Bog had ever seen. They gathered in the clearing under the rock platform where Small had announced Bog's triumph. Under the half-closed eye of the moon, trolls brought stools, stumps, anything to pull up to the long wooden tables strung together. And the food piled on those tables! Bog's nose twitched. He'd never smelled so much meat at once. Porcupine and fox. Barbequed mice on skewers. Roasted chicken, stolen from humans. Boiled goose eggs. Bowls of rich, steaming broth.

Sitting between Small and Frantsum, Bog ate his fill and then some more. With a stab of guilt, he thought of his family, hoping they were eating more than grubs and mousemeat stew.

As they ate, Small repeated his tale of Bog's victory over the loggers.

"Bog swept through the camp, swatting loggers left and right." Small demonstrated with his fist, making the trolls around him duck. "With each swipe, the loggers soared through the air and into the hollow reeking of wood spirits. They released their deadly fog on the humans, leaving only rot behind."

The forest trolls cheered. Bog shivered at the mention of rot. The story became more exaggerated with each telling.

Then the trolls talked of the goings-on near Thunder City.

"Watch out," a plump young troll said. "The Troll Hunter is taking down trolls, leaving a trail of statues and showing others how to do it, too."

Just like Josaya had warned. Bog shared the horror of Jeddal's stoning and explained how the humans had used the teachings of this Troll Hunter to do it.

Small's eyes were fierce. "This human is a monster."

"I heard he destroyed three mountain trolls at once." The plump troll shook his head. "His knife can cut through the toughest hide."

"He's hunted the mountain trolls to extinction, so now he's come here to practise his skills on us," added another.

"Mountain trolls extinct? Impossible." Small snorted.

"Where's the Troll Hunter now?" Bog asked.

"In Thunder City, we think." Frantsum picked at his food. "No one even knows his scent, since he destroys any who come near. Why do you want to know?" He leaned closer, examining Bog.

Bog shrugged. He hadn't told Small that he was after the Troll Hunter. These trolls might think him foolish.

When Bog could eat no more, he belched loudly and rubbed his greasy fingers clean on his stomach.

"Did you feed well enough?" Frantsum asked.

Bog answered with another large burp.

Frantsum shared a toothless grin. "And you drank your fill?"

Bog nodded. His stomach was bursting.

"Then it's time you pay for our hospitality," Frantsum announced in a raspy voice.

The trolls around them who heard let out a rowdy cheer.

Bog's tail became rigid. "I didn't know this feast came with a cost." If he'd known, he would have eaten nothing. Treasure was for hoarding, not trading.

He glanced at Small and the other furry faces around him—some smiling, some not so friendly— wondering how to get out of this jam.

"Of course there's a cost." Small grinned, showing pointed teeth with bits of meat still caught between them. He had the bones of an entire deer piled nearby.

"We always demand a story from our guests," Frantsum said. "It's the only payment we accept."

Bog blinked. "A story?"

Frantsum beamed. "Please, indulge an old troll. Climb onto the rock," he gestured toward the rock platform, "and tell me a story." He leaned back in his chair, his arms folded, his eyes expectant.

Bog began to sweat despite the cool night air. Telling stories was Kasha's skill, not his, and these forest trolls had unfamiliar ways. How could he ever please them?

The calls for a story began to swell, until the noise became deafening.

Bog's legs trembled, making his tail vibrate. Maybe he could tell one of Kasha's tales. The story of Ymir—his favourite. He knew the words by heart.

"Well?" Frantsum raised his bushy eyebrows. He was just a scrap of fur and bone, yet he had such authority, such kindness. Bog didn't want to refuse him.

He climbed onto the rock. Shouts and cheers buoyed him up. High above the other trolls, he prayed to Ymir for strength.

The trolls quieted, shifting in their seats, their eyes like weights on him. Bog gazed into the forest and launched into his story.

"In the beginning, there was no rock, no sea, no sun." The echo of Kasha's words fueled a yearning for his family. Bog tried to shake free of it, but it stuck like a burr. "There was only a hollow so vast that your mind would spin in circles if you tried to imagine it." Bog twirled his fingers, and a young troll who reminded Bog of Ruffan stood and began turning, until an older troll yanked him back down.

A few trolls chuckled.

Bog continued, his voice louder. "This dizzying space contained an icy mist and a fire too hot to hold life."

Frantsum smiled. Bog was relieved Kasha's words satisfied him.

"In the shimmering vapour where frost met spark, the first life formed." Bog paused, his arms outstretched. "This was Ymir, the frost giant—father of us all."

The crowd was still, taut with listening. Bog lifted his chin.

"Ymir was as wild as the mountains. Fiercer than a tempest. His breath was an icy blast." Then he said to the young troll who had spun in circles, "You would tremble before him."

The youngster roared. "I wouldn't be afraid."

Bog's tail wagged. Small chortled and then reached a long furry arm across the table to give the youngster a wallop.

"While Ymir slept, the race of frost giants sprang from his armpit. The world was fresh and new, trembling with life."

Shouts erupted from the crowd. Trolls stamped their feet and cheered.

"But this was not the only life to be formed from mist and fire." Bog's voice was a warning. "A smaller, weaker race took shape. They called themselves gods."

The crowd booed.

"The greatest of these gods was Odin, the Terrible One," Bog yelled, shaking his fist. "Odin and his brothers became jealous of Ymir's strength and courage. They pierced his hide until blood ran from his wounds, drowning most of Ymir's children."

"Murderers!" someone called.

"They were the first to kill." Bog nodded grimly. "From Ymir's skull they fashioned the sky. From his flesh the earth. From his bones the mountains. From his blood the sea."

"The body of Ymir is all around us!" another shouted.

"Yes." Bog's eyes misted over, as they always did at this part. "While the earth was still soft and alive with Ymir's last heartbeats," his voice was reverent, "a miracle happened."

The trolls became motionless, waiting as if they knew what was coming. Bog realized his story was familiar to these trolls, and the thought brought him closer to them. "As Ymir died, trolls sprang fully formed from his feet. It was a final gift from Ymir. A gift of hope for the world."

The clearing exploded with noise, as trolls stomped, howled, bellowed. Bog felt a rush of power. Like he could take on anything, even the Troll Hunter. High on this rock with the dark forest around him, he was so much more than a weak half-human.

When the racket faded, Bog spoke. "When Odin became jealous of the trolls, he created his own creatures to inhabit the land. He called them humans," Bog paused as the crowd jeered, "giving them souls that live forever, rather than letting them become one with Ymir upon death.

"Odin and his brothers ruled over the humans, who worshiped them. Then Odin cast a powerful magic upon all giants and trolls. He fashioned the sun to keep Ymir's offspring at bay. A sun whose light could turn giants and trolls to stone. This was Odin's curse." Bog paused, as Kasha usually did, letting the horror of the moment sink in. The trolls were with him—he could feel it. They hardly twitched, waiting for Bog's next words.

"Eventually, the gods and giants faded, but trolls and humans spilled from the northern mountains to inhabit the world." Bog spread his arms. "Mountain trolls, forest trolls, cave trolls—they adapted to life in different places. But all trolls spring from the original life—Ymir, the frost giant."

Bog punched the air. The crowd did, too. Bog saw an ocean of fists.

"Ymir! Ymir!" they chanted.

Then Bog caught sight of the human girl. She was sitting with the elderly troll, who was grooming the girl's hair and not even paying attention. A fierce cloud gathered inside Bog. As he stared, the girl locked eyes with him. She shook her fist and yelled Ymir's name.

How dare she listen to troll stories and learn their language! Jeddal had said, *Never let humans know anything about you. You never know when they'll use it against you.*

"We know that one night," Bog said, tearing his eyes away from the girl, "humans will destroy themselves through evil and foolishness. Then trolls will take their rightful place as rulers of the mountains, lakes, and forests that are the body of Ymir. We will not be limited to the darkness, but will rule both night and day."

Bog bowed. The forest trolls exploded once more. He made his way down off the rock and among the beaming furry faces, as many hands patted his back and many fists punched the air.

When Bog had found his way back to his seat, Frantsum said, "That was worth a meal." He grinned, showing his missing teeth.

Bog smiled so wide his cheeks hurt. Then he rubbed Frantsum's nose with his own, like he would an old friend's.

7

THE NOSE STONE

BOG jerked awake, banging his head on the low ceiling, a disturbing vision haunting him. Kasha and the youngsters—he had to take care of them. He glanced around, confused. Then he realized he was in Small's den, tunnelled into a sleeping burrow off the common room.

The burrow was just wider than Bog. It smelled of worms, earth, and the dried leaves that littered the floor. Bog rubbed his head and tried to find his warm spot among the leaves, cold with the evening's chill.

In his dream, Kasha had been twig thin, collapsed near the firepit in the lakeside cave. Ruffan was holding a bowl of broth to her lips. When he tipped the bowl to let her drink, she let the liquid dribble into her chin fur.

"Has Bog returned?" Her voice was raspy.

Ruffan shook his head sadly. "Maybe tomorrow night."

Bog propped himself up. Was Ruffan hunting well? Did they have enough to eat? Bog missed the familiar sleeping nook he shared with Ruffan, and this strange burrow just wasn't right without the youngster's scent.

He crawled into the common room, still distracted by the dream. Was it telling him to return home?

Not without defeating the Troll Hunter.

In the common room, Bog could see signs of wealth that he hadn't noticed before. The wooden table was inlaid with polished stone, and the pantry cupboard was still full after last night's feast. Even the lynx half-asleep by the fire meant food was plentiful.

Bog caught a whiff of Frantsum's woody scent. Again, Bog hadn't noticed him tucked into his corner near the fire, looking like a rumpled mound of earth. As Bog greeted him, Frantsum began to chuckle, which led to a fit of coughing.

Bog hurried to pour him some cold broth from a clay jug on the table, thinking how he should be caring for Kasha this way.

He helped the old troll to drink. When Frantsum recovered, he sputtered his thanks. "I still enjoy the idea of those loggers turned to rot by wood spirits," he said with a chortle, his voice hoarse. "You're a cunning troll, Bog."

Bog returned the jug to the table. "I hope I'm cunning enough."

"Cunning enough for what?" Frantsum perked up. "Why are you travelling? Where are you going? I'm sorry to pry, but…" He leaned forward. "Small is determined to fulfill his *gnark*, and I want to know what he's pledging himself to."

Bog sucked in a breath. He couldn't avoid the topic any longer.

"Fair enough." He tromped over to a chair at the table and sat down.

Just then, Small lurched into the room, heavy with sleep. "Good nightfall to you." He scratched his furry belly and rummaged in the pantry cupboard.

"Good nightfall, Small." Bog watched him pull out a gaudy blue-and-red box with squiggly human symbols on it.

"Ymir is smiling on you, Bog." Small cheerfully waved the box. "I'm about to introduce you to the fine taste of hamburgers, courtesy of the human grocery store."

Bog nodded. The meat inside the box did smell delicious, although it was starting to turn.

Frantsum stared at Bog expectantly.

Bog traced the woodgrain of the tabletop with his fingernail, avoiding Frantsum's gaze. "I'm looking for someone."

"Who? A forest troll?" Small said. He was stirring the few coals in the fireplace, adding twigs and small branches. A stream of smoke began to rise toward a hole in the roof.

"Not exactly." Bog shook his head. "Not a troll."

"Then…a human?" Frantsum's eyes were steady.

Small put the hamburgers on to cook, releasing a rich scent into the room.

"Yes. I need to find the Troll Hunter—he turned my father to stone. I mean, he helped. Like I told you last night, he…he taught other humans how to trick us."

"Not to be harsh," Frantsum paused, "but why seek the Troll Hunter when your father is already stone?"

Bog squirmed. "To protect my family—and other trolls who may be hunted." He tried to keep the indignant tone from his voice.

Frantsum tugged at the fur on his chin. "Not to avenge your father?"

Bog found his hands clenched and made them relax. *Don't hoard your anger as if it's gold. It's not troll-like,* Kasha had said. "Of course not," Bog forced through his teeth.

Frantsum nodded. "Protecting your family is a noble quest."

Bog was relieved Frantsum asked nothing more.

He breathed in the scent of the cooking hamburgers, and his stomach began to grumble. How could he be hungry after last night's feast?

"You've helped us banish the loggers," Frantsum said, "and I want to return the favour. Do you know the legend of the Nose Stone?"

"No," Bog began, hoping to avoid a long story. "But I did want to ask about—"

"It's not common," Frantsum continued. "A few forest trolls from the south shared it with me once. You might find it interesting."

"Actually, I was hoping you could tell me where to—"

"Just listen." Frantsum waved his pointed fingernails in Bog's face. "This story is about a giant named Sideways. He lived in an underwater cave in Superior Lake, far to the south, near Thunder City."

Bog crossed his arms and tried to pay attention.

"Sideways was peculiar," Frantsum's voice crackled, "because he made friends with a group of humans. For some fool reason, he believed these humans were different than most. Upright like trees." Frantsum rolled his eyes.

"Is this the one about—" Small began.

"Shush." Frantsum cut him off with another wave of his hand. "Sideways told these humans dangerous secrets. He even shared his hoard with them." Frantsum shook his head. "Unthinkable, isn't it? He shared his treasure in exchange for a favour."

Bog nodded, unsure where this story was headed.

"For his part, Sideways told them where to find a vein of silver in a series of caves on an island in Superior Lake. In return, he asked them to hide a most valuable treasure within one of those caves, where his big hands couldn't reach. He had those humans conceal the blessed Nose of Ymir—safe from thieves. Not the whole nose—that would be too massive to hide anywhere—but just the nub, warts and all.

"These humans lived well, becoming known for their silver ornaments. Soon, other humans wanted the silver, too. They sent a scout to learn the location of the mine. When the scout discovered it, he gathered the largest pieces he could carry and then set off for home." Frantsum lowered his voice. "But on the way, he was set upon by three other men, who forced him to reveal the source of the silver.

"At once, the men headed for the mine by canoe, singing loudly about the riches they'd enjoy. Their noise alerted Sideways. As they approached the mine entrance, Sideways rose out of the water, causing a mighty wave to batter the shore. But, in his haste, Sideways didn't realize it was almost sunrise. He emerged from the lake as the sun rose above the hills." Frantsum grimaced.

Bog gritted his teeth as the whole terrible moment with Jeddal came crashing back. "Why are you telling me this?"

"Just wait." Frantsum raised both hands.

Small was motionless, listening. The hamburgers sizzled and smoked.

"The sun, in her wretched glory, turned poor Sideways to stone, and he fell with a mighty splash into the lake." Frantsum slapped a hand on his thigh. "And there he rests to this night—on his back in the water, majestic in death."

Bog blinked hard, trying not to think of Jeddal.

"Sideways was desperate to protect the Nose Stone." Frantsum spoke in a hushed tone, leaning forward, his eyes searching Bog's. "We all know how sacred a nose is, how it tells so much about a troll."

Bog raised a hand to hide his own blunt nose.

"But Ymir's Nose Stone had special properties—the power to revive a giant or troll who has been turned to stone."

"What?" Bog's legs began to tremble. His hand fell.

"When placed on the head of a stone troll while the moon is rising in the sky, the Nose Stone will make them flesh again. But the troll must be whole, not a chip missing." Frantsum leaned back, a satisfied look on his face. "That's what made me think of you and your father."

Jeddal. Could Bog save him? His head reeled. "Is... this true?"

"I'm not sure how much is truth and how much is rumour." Frantsum shrugged. "Many have searched for the Nose Stone, but no one has found it. The story goes that you can still see the mine entrance on Silver Island at the foot of the Sleeping Giant. Humans unearthed the silver until the lake took revenge, filling their tunnels with water. The Sleeping Giant guards his treasure well—although some say he showed those humans a hidden entrance into the mine from the mainland shore."

"You never mentioned the hidden entrance before." Small flipped the hamburgers onto a platter, one by one.

"Didn't I?" Frantsum scratched his chin. "The talk is that the hidden entrance looks like a stone with three mouths, and the middle mouth leads to the mine. But no one can find it. Maybe it's overgrown. Maybe it collapsed. Maybe it never existed."

"Hamburgers for everyone." Small placed the platter piled high with disks of meat on the table and then smacked Bog hard on the shoulder. "So what is our quest—Troll Hunter or Nose Stone?"

The scent of the hamburgers choked Bog. He would rather save Jeddal, yet was it possible?

A mythical stone underneath a lake. It was too ridiculous to hope for. Yet Ymir's nose had to be somewhere.

Bog's hands were shaking and his stomach was too tangled to eat. Small watched him, waiting. Frantsum hobbled over to the table, his eyes fixed on the meat.

Bog pushed back from the table, unsure what to do. If he didn't try to rescue Jeddal, he'd regret it forever. But what if the Nose Stone was just a story? The longer the Troll Hunter was alive, the more trolls would suffer. He'd already delayed his quest by taking down a logging camp and feasting with forest trolls.

"We need to stop the Troll Hunter first," Bog said to Small's questioning face. "Then we can find the

Nose Stone." If it existed.

Small let out a whoop. "We're hunting us a Troll Hunter." He smacked his fist on the table, rattling the platter.

Frantsum frowned. "May Ymir guide you well." He sank his few remaining teeth into a hamburger.

8

THE HUMAN

Inside Frantsum's lair, Bog checked his rucksack one more time and then tightened the drawstring to close it. When he hoisted it, the string cut into his shoulder. Although he appreciated Small's packets of dried fish and the jug of broth, he was determined never to wear the human clothes Small had made him pack, even as a disguise.

Bog had spent most of the previous night with Small and Frantsum, planning their route to Thunder City and brainstorming how to trick the Troll Hunter once they found him. Although Small and Frantsum had plotted ways to trap the Troll Hunter, Bog had silently vowed to destroy him. Now, he resettled the bulging rucksack on his shoulder and turned to Small, impatient to set off.

"Ready to go?" He'd enjoy Small's company and

make good use of his strength.

Small lifted his own rucksack, which was twice as large as Bog's. "I wouldn't miss it." His eyes shone in the firelight.

Bog emerged from Frantsum's lair with Small behind him as the last rays of sunlight faded from view. He raised his eyebrows at the collection of forest trolls, headed by Frantsum, that had gathered in the thick shadows under the trees. The young troll who had called out during Bog's story, the plump troll who'd talked about the Troll Hunter, and most of the others—had they all come to see them off?

"May Ymir bless your journey," called out the plump troll.

"The Troll Hunter's in for trouble," yelled another.

Then a cheer rose from the crowd, warming Bog to the tip of his tail. He'd never had such a send-off.

"Be careful around humans," Frantsum warned as the noise died down. His tight mouth reminded Bog of his farewell with Kasha.

"I'm always safe." Small whacked his father—not too hard—on the shoulder.

They said their goodbyes, bumping noses with Frantsum and yanking each forest troll's nose. How friendly these trolls had become; maybe Bog had more in common with them than he'd thought. Finally, Bog and Small made their way through the settlement, among the hunters preparing for the night and youngsters wrestling in the dirt.

Near the edge of the settlement, Small stopped

before the old female troll who'd coddled the human girl. The troll was hunched over, weeping. Bog was grateful that the girl was nowhere in sight.

"Where is she, Diama?" Small demanded.

Diama looked up. Her eyes were rheumy, and her nose red.

"What's going on?" Bog asked Small. He hoped the girl had already been traded away. But Diama raised a skinny finger to point at the entrance to a burrow.

The girl emerged, watery-eyed and sallow, dragging a gaudy pink rucksack. In the moonlight, her hair shone ghostly white, her skin was pallid, and her eyes were grey. She wore clothes and shoes, although her legs and arms were bare. Worst of all, her scent stung Bog's nose, making his eyes water.

"She can't be coming…" Bog shook his head.

"We're trading for her in Strongarm," Small said. "It's on the way, more or less."

Bog scowled, willing it not to be true.

Small settled a heavy hand on Bog's shoulder. "She's like a walking sack of information and supplies, although we may not get as much for her this time, since it's our second trade with this girl."

"But can't someone else—" Bog began.

"Think about it, Bog. What if we could use her to find out exactly where the Troll Hunter's den is?"

Bog fumed silently. Small was right.

Diama and the girl clutched each other, yanking noses and blubbering farewells. It sickened Bog— hearing the girl speak troll language and seeing her embrace a troll. Didn't Small realize she was dangerous?

"Don't take Hannie from me." The old troll whimpered.

"Please," Hannie begged Small, still clinging to Diama. "Let me stay."

"Come on." Small jerked the girl away and tossed her onto his shoulder. "You've stayed too long."

Diama wailed. The girl struggled uselessly.

Bog couldn't watch. He turned to the forest, not even waiting for Small to point the way.

Bog worked his way through balsam fir and white pine, always keeping ahead of Small and the girl. She polluted the air by talking non-stop in troll talk with a few human words woven in when she got stuck. First, she begged to return to the troll settlement, next she sobbed, and then she begged some more. When she finally gave up, she lay draped over Small's shoulder, flopping along on her stomach with each step he took. How could Small bear to touch her?

"Keep to the left up there," Small called. "We'll skirt the lake and save ourselves some time."

It was a two-night walk to Strongarm, and Bog was dreading every moment. All because of Hannie—he didn't want to know her name or even speak to her, but she kept yakking, abusing the troll language.

"Have you ever seen a giant?" she asked Small.

"No. None left, that I know of, unless they're farther north or in the western mountains." Small didn't seem to mind her endless questions.

"Do all trolls dream?"

"Yeah. I dreamed about a crow that could talk last night."

"What do you do with your silver?" Hannie swatted the mosquitoes that buzzed around her.

"Count it."

"Why?"

"To see how much there is."

"How long do trolls live?"

"Oh, about twice as long as humans."

Bog's tail twitched. Why did Small answer? And why was she so keen to learn about trolls?

"What happens to trolls when they die?" Hannie asked.

Not that.

Bog surged ahead, away from her voice, away from the answer that Small would give. But the memory of Jeddal's stoning had already resurfaced, and he couldn't outrun it.

But you're going to do something about it, Bog told himself. *After you destroy the Troll Hunter, you'll find the Nose Stone, if it's real, and make its magic work.*

Then Jeddal would explain everything—why he mated with a human, and why he never told Bog about it.

Bog trudged along, keeping far enough from

Hannie that he could almost forget about her. He watched the position of the stars when he could glimpse them through the trees, checking that he was still travelling southwest. The forest was muted by shadow, and Bog sensed his way through the darkness, nostrils flaring. A hare had crossed this way—the scent was fading. And it had rained there yesterday.

Then the forest opened into a rare clearing, dominated by a rocky crest. As he found his footing among the loose rocks, he contemplated the moon, high above the ridge. Ymir's eye, many called it, watching over trolls. The moon was white with grey patches and just over half full. It gazed down, its bluish light revealing the shrubs, mosses, and lichen that embraced the rough and tumbled rock. The ridge had been a mountain once, vast and towering. Although climbing it made Bog's breath quicken, it was just a small swelling of its ancient glory.

Bog sat on a north-facing ledge near the weather-beaten summit with his tail out behind. He pulled out a jug of broth and a hunk of dried fish. Small and Hannie would catch up, but his stomach was gurgling and his legs had begun to ache. Bog wondered how far he'd walked since he'd left Kasha, and how many more steps until he'd return home.

He bit into the fish, his stomach anticipating it with a growl. The forest lay like a furry pelt, dark and accepting, until Small and Hannie emerged with Hannie still talking. He forced himself to chew and swallow, even though her scent made him nauseated.

The girl was walking now—an elf beside Small, her ears sticking out through her long pale hair. Her bright-pink rucksack hung off one shoulder.

"Even though sight is a troll's weakest sense," Small said as they climbed the rocks side by side, "it's still better than a human's feeble eyesight."

"I knew that." In one hand, she clutched a gaudy doll.

"Stop telling her about us." Bog frowned. "She could use it to trick us."

Hannie held up the doll. "Look at my troll doll. Her name's Thunder."

She held a disgusting plastic toy. Garish blue fur sprouted from its head, and a jewel in its belly button peeked out from between its human clothes. How dare she mock trolls with that doll?

"She won't remember much." Small gave Bog a friendly punch. "Humans aren't so smart. And we might learn something useful from her."

"Troll ways are none of her concern." Bog scowled.

"I knew nothing about trolls until they took me." Hannie's grey eyes widened. "I was scared at first, but it was better than home. So after they sent me home, I sneaked back. It was hard, and I got lost a lot. But I'll do it again. I belong with trolls."

"No, you don't." Bog silently counted the nights until he'd be free of her.

"You made it back to the settlement by yourself?" Small shook his head, an amazed expression on his face.

"All by myself." Hannie beamed. "Until Diama found me. She carried me then." Her hair fell away from her face when she lifted her head to Small. "Diama's nice, not like my dad. She reminds me of my Aunt Rachel who moved far away," she babbled on. "Now I only have my dad since my mom died when I was little." Her face was pale in the moonlight, emphasizing the dark shadows around her eyes. "Dad's always telling me I'm no good. He didn't even look for me when I was gone. He said Aunt Rachel left because of how no-good I am, but I don't believe him. I think she left because she was a troll. That's why my dad hates me—because I'm a troll, too."

"No!" Bog leapt up. He'd heard enough. He started shoving his belongings into his rucksack.

"You have no tail." Small pointed out. "Or fur."

Bog gaped at Small. "How can you even discuss this with her?"

"But I can hear real well." Hannie pleaded like she needed them to believe her. "And smell good, too."

Bog dug his fingernails into his palms. "You are not a troll!" His bellow silenced the crickets.

"Bog, calm down." Small stepped between them.

Hannie peeked around Small. Her eyes were

watery again. "Why don't you like me?" Her chin quivered. "I like you. I want to be just like you when I'm big. Strong. Brave. Not afraid of anything."

"You…you…" Bog's legs trembled. She was a pathetic human. But he was hardly better.

Bog turned from Small and the girl.

"You'll never be like me," he said. But he wasn't so sure.

Bog shouldered his rucksack and set off toward Strongarm.

9

A FOREIGN WORLD

BOG had walked farther into human territory than ever before. He could smell the difference already.

The evening breeze carried the stench of gasoline mixed with smoke that burned his nostrils. Putrid pools of water choked out plant life near the railway track. A husk of a car reeked of rust in a forest glen.

Human sounds invaded, too. The distant buzz of machines cutting down trees, speeding along roads, thundering across the sky. The rumble of a train, and the painful whistle blast.

Bog walked until his feet throbbed and then he walked even more, always assaulted by the scents and sounds of humans, especially Hannie.

Small seemed to understand how Bog felt about Hannie, although they never talked about her.

Sometimes, Bog trudged behind them to avoid her constant nattering. Or he linked up with them after he'd soothed his ears with the fury of a waterfall or the rush of winds through creaking branches. During the day, he slept apart, shivering alone because he couldn't bear her scent up close.

After two whole nights, Bog found himself ahead of Hannie and Small, alone in a cluster of slender birches, glaring up at a yellow plastic bag caught high among the branches. The wind had torn the bag into strips. Twigs poked holes through it. Yet somehow, it endured.

Bog growled deep in his throat. How dare the bag lodge in this birch like some sickly flag claiming territory for humans?

He shook the tree, but the bag stuck fast. He tried to climb to pull it down, but the thin branches bent under his weight. He shook a fist at it. The bag fluttered in the breeze. Lit up from behind by the moon's rays, it gleamed like a false sun.

"It's a Haliday's bag," Hannie announced, suddenly at his elbow.

"What?" Bog jumped. How had she sneaked up on him?

"From the grocery store beside the gas station." Hannie glanced at Bog and then added, "It's a place to get food and stuff."

"Where?" asked Small from behind her, sniffing the air. Their supplies were low after two nights of walking, and Small had cut back on his gigantic portions. "I don't smell a grocery store."

"There's no grocery store, just a bag from one." Hannie laughed.

Small chuckled, too.

"Let's just find a place for the day." Bog turned from the bag and their laughter.

They stopped outside Strongarm just before sunrise. Small slipped away to survey the town from the forest's edge. Bog found a deep crevice under a rock overhang where they could shelter. He didn't have time to hunt before sunrise, but he hadn't hunted successfully since Jeddal had been turned to stone. Small returned with a bag from a garbage bin—another place to get human food—and they sorted through the rubbish. Bog couldn't believe the meat these humans threw away. Didn't they think about tomorrow's breakfast?

Once Hannie fell asleep against the rock, clutching her offensive troll doll, Small began to whisper plans.

"I want you to take the girl back to her father—see what you can trade for her."

"Me? But I thought—"

"It's simple—just disguise yourself as a human so you can get into town without a pack of troll hunters noticing. You can pass as a human more easily, Bog." Small settled his bulk into an earthy hollow near Hannie. "You're shorter. No fur on your face. And your nose is almost human-sized."

Bog flinched. "What are you saying?"

"That I'm too big to pass for a human. I've tried it

before, but they get suspicious."

"I can't masquerade as a human." Bog found a sleeping spot near the overhang's edge, as far away from Hannie as he could get. "It's too…" Close to the truth.

"Of course you can. I can't wait to see you walking their streets without any fool human noticing." Small chuckled. "After you find the girl's father, you just make demands in exchange for her safe return. You can ask about the location of the Troll Hunter's den, or for food…" he suggested, licking his lips, "…or gold, jewels, money. Get as much as you can for her, and then get out. I'll stay in the shadows, in case of trouble."

"Can't we just storm in and crush any humans who—"

"And end up with hundreds of them hunting us? No. This is the best way."

"I suppose." Bog glanced at Hannie, who was sleeping peacefully. "I can't wait to get rid of her."

"What do you have against her?"

"What do you mean? She's human."

"I know, but any human is good for something—"

"Even the Troll Hunter?" Bog growled. "Is he good for something?"

Small's eyes lingered on Bog's clenched fists and then searched his face. "The Troll Hunter is a menace." He nodded slowly. His furry brow wrinkled.

Bog forced his hands to relax, trying not to act like a revenge-filled human. He pretended to stretch and yawn. "We'll stop the Troll Hunter. Then we'll go to the Sleeping Giant, find that Nose Stone, and rescue Jeddal."

The day was too muggy to sleep. By evening, it was still humid.

"The sun is almost down," Hannie announced. She was shadow-slipping, as if the sun's rays might harm her.

Small draped a yellow plastic coat over Bog's shoulders. "This should work."

The coat trapped Bog's sweat. "I can't wear this… thing." He threw off the coat, disgusted by the scent of the last human who'd worn it.

"It's called a raincoat. And it's a great disguise." Small grinned, plopping a matching hat with a floppy brim onto Bog's head and then handing him a pair of black rain pants.

Bog pulled the hat off and threw it to the ground. "Tuck in my tail? Play-act being a human? I've changed my mind. I can't do this."

Small rescued the hat and coat and then eyed Bog. "You've never been in a town before, have you?"

"Of course not. Why would I want to?"

"A lot of humans live there. More than you'd expect. If you walk through a town without wearing clothes, they'll attack. That's why we always disguise ourselves until we make the trade."

"If I wear that plastic thing, they'll smell me coming."

"Humans can't smell so good," Hannie said, beside Bog now. "And you'll look cute, even though it's not raining." She reached up and patted Bog's arm.

He yanked away. "Don't touch me! Never touch me!" He ignored Hannie's withered look. "Isn't there another way to trade?" he asked Small.

"This is the best way." Small offered the clothes once more. "Just take her in and see what you can get for her."

"I'll help you get stuff," Hannie announced, "but I'm not going back to my dad. I heard you talking last night. You want to find the Troll Hunter and then visit the Sleeping Giant, right? I can help you. I know I can."

"You were supposed to be asleep." Bog growled.

"I was just pretending. What's a Nose Stone? Who's Jeddal?"

"None of your business." Bog let his voice rise, hoping to scare her. "And you're not coming. You're going back to your father and you're never returning to the forest troll camp again. Do you understand?"

Tears welled up in Hannie's eyes. "I'd rather stay with you."

It took a while for Small to calm Bog and Hannie down. He convinced Bog that he needed to tolerate the clothes long enough to work their plan. But

Small couldn't convince Hannie that she had to stay with her father.

"I'm coming with you." She pouted, her arms folded across her chest.

Finally, Small whispered to Bog, "She'll probably go easily once she gets home. They always do. Just leave her there. We'll be gone before she notices."

They packed the last of the broth and meat as the sun set. Then they set off for Strongarm. Small shadow-slipped through the forest. Bog and Hannie hiked straight down the road that led into town.

In the rain pants, coat, and hat, Bog was stiflingly hot. Sweat trickled down the inside of the plastic and soaked his matted fur. His tail was squished uncomfortably down one leg of the pants, and he wanted to twitch it free.

"Why do humans wear this stuff?" he muttered.

At least his feet hadn't fit the human shoes, although the pants covered most of his feet.

The trees began to thin. Trimmed grass replaced the forest undergrowth. The road became smooth tar and stone, rather than rough dirt. Too flat. Unnatural. The road held the sun's warmth, heating the bottom of Bog's feet. He stepped lightly, although his pants made a swishing noise as he walked. Hannie's shoes flapped against the road.

Had Martinique Bottom dressed Bog in clothes? A disturbing idea. He studied the surrounding landscape, trying to force a memory of where he'd once lived with his parents. In a cave near Strongarm? Not in a building, he hoped.

The clouds blotted out the stars. Bog couldn't believe he was walking into Strongarm, dressed as one of them. He wanted to trade Hannie as fast as possible.

Hannie chattered beside him, scampering to keep up. "I've been gone for days and days now. Last time, my teacher was the only one who noticed I was gone. She always asks questions about my dad, but I don't answer in case he gets mad. And every day she wants me to do math, but the numbers get stuck inside my head—"

"Quiet," Bog said. "We don't want to be noticed."

"Okay, I'll be quiet, Bog. You can count on me." She shut her mouth, nodding eagerly.

He doubted it would last.

More and more buildings appeared, and signs with strange markings that he couldn't decipher. Bright lights on tall poles illuminated everything, blinding Bog to the nuances within the shadows. Moths and other insects swarmed the lights, confused by the human-made moons.

Bog felt just as lost. The buildings were everywhere. Short wooden ones and much taller stone ones. He could smell hundreds of humans inside. The reek was almost overwhelming. Small had been right. It was no place for a troll.

His throat tightened. He sniffed behind to make sure they weren't being followed. Was Small nearby? He couldn't smell him. Maybe he should turn back.

Then a car appeared ahead of them, its lights blinding. Within moments, another approached from behind. Bog's hands grew clammy. His knees locked. Was a pack of troll hunters surrounding him? He could imagine what they'd do to him.

The cars sped closer. Hannie's tiny fingers tugged at his sleeve, pulling him sideways.

"Don't stand in the middle of the road." Her voice was shrill. "Do you want to get run over?"

Bog stumbled after her. Both cars slowed beside them, rumbling like thunder. Music throbbed from one—a reminder of the puny man with the noise box. Bog pulled away from Hannie, covering his ears. His head threatened to burst apart.

"Stay off the road," a man called through the racket, speaking in the awkward human language.

They know, Bog thought. *They're coming for me.*

"You think it's gonna rain, buddy?" came another voice, followed by jeering laughter.

"Leave him alone!" Hannie yelled.

Then the noise began to fade. The cars were pulling away, leaving their stench behind. Bog freed his ears. His breathing was quick. He tried to calm down, telling himself that he was safe, for now.

"What were you doing?" Hannie gaped. "Why did you stop on the road?"

"Too loud," was all Bog said, turning from her. "Where's your home?" She saved him from those cars, much like he'd saved Small. Did he owe her a *gnark*? Impossible.

"Up ahead." Hannie gave him a puzzled look.

They hurried past darkened buildings. Only a few windows were lit up. Bog skirted the pools of light from the streetlamps, cowering at the slightest noise.

"That's where I went to school." Hannie pointed to a brick building, forgetting her promise to be quiet. "My teacher was Mrs. Phelps. She has puffy blonde hair. But I don't belong there because I'm really a troll. That's why the kids made fun of me."

Bog tried to block out her chatter.

"There's the food store I told you about," Hannie continued. "I buy white freezies there when I get money. White freezies taste like all the other flavours put together." She pointed down a road with smaller buildings. "We go this way."

Bog's stomach churned his breakfast. The town seemed endless. How could there be enough stone, wood, and metal to make so many buildings and cars? He thought about Hannie rescuing him from those cars, and suddenly he wanted to leave his mark in this vast human town, just to prove he could. He paused beside a street sign on a tall metal post.

"Stop," Bog ordered Hannie.

He pushed against the post, straining every muscle in his body. The post slowly bent toward the road.

"What are you doing?" Hannie asked. "Why are you breaking that sign?"

Bog pushed until the sign was twisted into the

road where it would block a car. Then he smacked the post, saying the words to shape-shimmer it. Both the sign and post became invisible. Bog smiled.

"Where did it go? How'd you do that?" Hannie gaped. "You sure are strong."

"Which way did you say your home was?" Bog felt ready to face her father.

"This way." Hannie pointed. "Can you teach me how to do that?"

"Come on." Bog set a faster pace. He'd be rid of her soon.

They hurried down streets and between buildings. Bog tried not to imagine swarms of troll hunters suddenly emerging from a darkened building, or more cars coming at him.

"Here's my house," Hannie announced.

Bog stared at it, uneasy about entering a human's den. Hannie dug her troll doll out of her rucksack and clutched it to her chest. The house was smaller than others on the street, with a black roof and white wooden slats covering the outside walls. The windows were dark except for the large rectangular one. A bluish light flickered from it.

"He's watching TV in the living room." Hannie's voice trembled. "Be careful."

TV? Living room? The way she said *be careful* made Bog wonder what he was walking into. But he'd come this far, so he marched up the concrete walk, climbed the wooden stairs, crossed the creaky porch, and banged open the door with his shoulder.

The room reeked of sour fruit. A glowing box in the far corner buzzed with human nattering. A table and chairs filled half the room. And one large man was scrunched down in a cushioned chair.

The man was almost as big as Bog. His nose was pitiful—small and flat in his rounded, startled face. He was wearing a white shirt and grey shorts, and his smell nearly knocked Bog flat. This man was the source of the sour-fruit smell. Several bottles on the floor beside his chair stank of it, too.

"What the…?" The man stood, wobbling slightly. The muscles in his arm flexed and rippled as he made a fist. "You sure are one ugly troll."

Bog panicked—the man knew he was a troll—and then recovered. This man was just a human. Bog could do this.

Hannie peeked around Bog's leg. "Go get him, Bog," she whispered.

"You back?" The man sneered at Hannie. "I thought you were gone for good this time."

Bog just wanted to dump Hannie and leave, but Small was counting on him to trade. In one quick movement, he snatched Hannie up by her rucksack and dangled her out front. "Tell me where to find the Troll Hunter or she gets hurt."

Hannie yelped and then shook her doll at her father. "You'd better answer him!" she yelled. "He's meaner than the last one."

"How should I know where the Troll Hunter is?" The man scowled at Bog. "And even if I did, I wouldn't tell the likes of you. I don't care how many of you no-souls get killed. Now get outta my house."

He came at Bog, fists ready.

Bog dropped Hannie.

She thudded to the floor and scuttled out of the way.

Bog's heart hammered in his chest. *Ymir, help me,* he thought.

10

RESCUE

Hannie's father barrelled closer, limping slightly. Bog's blood pounded.

"His knee! Get his knee!" Hannie yelled from beside the glowing box. "He hurt it at work before he got so—Bog, watch out!"

Bog let the rain hat slide off his head. He dropped one shoulder and twisted so it collided with the man's chest. The blow vibrated through Bog's body and he stepped back, although he refused to flinch. He saw surprise in the man's eyes, just before Bog jerked his fist up into the man's chin, the movement ripping the sleeve off his raincoat at the shoulder. The man gurgled as his head flipped up. Bog then kicked the man's weak knee. The man let out an ear-splitting yell and then collapsed backward onto the floor. Bog heaved a breath and yanked the torn sleeve from his arm, grateful to have it off.

Hannie scrambled to her father, her hands and knees slipping on the dusty wooden floor. "Dad?" she called, a catch in her voice.

He didn't move. Bog wondered if Hannie would cry, but she began clawing at the side of her father's shorts.

"What are you doing?" Bog's every muscle was taut, ready for the man to rise.

Hannie dug in her father's pocket until she smiled triumphantly, withdrawing a wad of useless paper wrapped in a tight roll.

"What good is that?" Bog snorted.

"Money." Hannie trilled like a songbird announcing the sunrise. "For Small."

"Oh." She was quick-witted, for a human.

Then a muscled arm snaked from behind Hannie and wrapped around her middle.

"Steal from your own kin?" Her father's twisted face appeared over her shoulder. "I always knew you were no good!"

"Catch, Bog!" Hannie threw the money roll.

Bog snagged it in mid-air and shoved it deep into the pocket of his rain pants.

"Why you worthless brat!" her father bellowed, squeezing her in his hold.

Hannie squealed, struggling to free herself.

Bog stumbled backward, trying to ignore the urge to rip the man's arm off Hannie. Rescue a human? Ridiculous. Bog ducked through the doorway and onto the creaky wooden porch, letting the door swing shut.

"Bog! Don't leave me!" Hannie cried from inside the house.

He headed down the porch steps. Even if her father was a vile creature who didn't care for his young, it wasn't Bog's concern. He couldn't owe Hannie a *gnark*.

A crash from the house made Bog spin around.

"Hannie!" He howled into the night and then wished he hadn't.

Bog found himself racing back to the house. He banged the door open so hard that it lodged itself in the wall.

Hannie trembled behind the box, her pink rucksack still strapped to her shoulders. Hannie's father stood by the table and chairs, glowering.

"I told you to get out," her father bellowed at Bog. His neck was knotted cords of muscle. His face a sweaty, gleaming mass.

Hannie's eyes darted between them.

"Leave her alone." Bog stretched to his full height, growling.

Hannie's father picked up a chair and threw it at Bog's head.

Bog swatted the chair, forcing it off to the side. It smashed into the corner of the wall and broke apart. Before Bog could attack, Hannie's father was in his face, smashing a bottle over his nose. Mucus filled Bog's nostrils until he could smell nothing. He snorted in the phlegm, ignored the flowering pain, and focused only on his target.

Bog charged into the man with his full weight. He struck a blow to the man's face with his head. His hands searched for a grip. The man's skin was slick with sweat, slippery and smooth. Bog latched onto one leg and arm while the man was still dazed from the blow. He lifted the man into the air, spinning as he grappled with the weight, his tail jammed into his pants, unable to help him balance. He swung closer to the large front window and heaved the man through it. The glass shattered into the night as the man tumbled onto the porch.

Somewhere outside, a dog began to bark.

Hannie raced outside to where her father lay. Bog followed. Her father blinked and tried to lift his head. His nose was bleeding. Blood dribbled from small cuts on his arms and legs.

"You mean, mean man!" Hannie shrieked. "You're not my dad anymore. I'm leaving. I'm going to the Sleeping Giant with Bog. And even after we find the Nose Stone, I'm not coming back. Not ever!"

"No!" Bog roared. He'd rescued her for this?

Lights popped on in the next house, illuminating the grass and street.

Bog squinted. More lights from other houses. The sound of voices and footsteps. Where was Small?

He stumbled down the stairs and onto the grass. Hannie pursued him like a wolf to its prey.

"Bog, wait! I'm coming, too. Don't leave!"

"No!" Bog spun around, wondering which way to run.

A long wail pierced the night. Painfully loud, even from a distance.

Hannie gasped. "The police are coming."

"Small!" Bog called, lurching onto the road. The lights from the windows hurt his eyes. His ears throbbed with the wailing noise. His nose ached more than he thought possible.

He staggered away from the source of the sound. Lights hit him from behind. He glanced back. His eyes watered at the flashing red-and-white beams from an approaching car.

"Bog!" Hannie was still calling, following.

"Can't see." Bog swiped at the tears, stumbling forward. The sounds and the lights confused him. His nose throbbed. He spun sideways away from the car and loped toward a murky passage between two houses.

"Please, Small," Bog pleaded to his absent friend. "Don't let me be caught like this."

"Run! This way, Bog!" Small's voice. Finally.

Bog turned, not sure where Small was or when he might smack into a tree or building. His eyes still streamed. His head pulsed. He jogged after Small's scent the best he could with his injured, stuffy nose, stumbling over roads and grasses, smashing through bushes, straining to hear the padding of Small's feet over the wail of the car. He tore the rest of the raincoat from his back and scuttled faster in the clumsy pants.

Moments later, he caught a whiff of the forest—the scent of pine and balsam, of decaying leaves and new growth, of squirrels and mice. The wailing was farther away. Bog's ears slowly stopped ringing.

Bog welcomed the darkness, shadow-slipping with Small among the rocks and trees until all human sounds and scents were indistinct, except for Hannie's. He glanced back to see her trailing, her rucksack slung over one shoulder.

Finally, Small halted. "You all right?" He wasn't even short of breath after the run.

Bog nodded, crumpling against the trunk of a birch, wiping his eyes and nose. He felt his nose for damage. It was swollen and tender.

"Sorry about that." Small leaned over to examine Bog's nose. "I never expected it would get rough. I was trying to keep an eye on you, but I couldn't stay close without being seen."

Bog shrugged Small away. "I'm fine." He wrenched off the rain pants. The roll of money fell between him and Small. Bog picked it up and handed it over. "At least we got this."

"Really? The plan worked?" Small tossed the money in the air and then caught it again, just as Hannie stumbled through the undergrowth, breathing hard.

"Sort of." Bog inhaled a wad of phlegm, tasting blood.

Hannie fell to her knees at Bog's feet, scrapes all over her arms and legs. "Oh, Bog, thank you, thank you, thank you for rescuing me. No one has ever helped with my dad before. You're a hero. I'm so glad I'm coming with you."

Bog stepped back. "You're not." After what he'd endured, any *gnark* he might have owed her had been paid.

"But you can't send me back. My dad's awful mad now. I'll do anything. Really. I can be good. I helped get the money, right? Please? I'll leave you alone. I'll never talk to you. I'll never touch you." Hannie wiped a hand across her watery eyes. "Please, Bog, I don't want to go back."

Bog shuddered and glanced at Small.

"I'm not sure what happened," Small tilted his head to one side, "but I bet the story is a good one."

"It was…not what I expected." Bog couldn't admit how he'd saved Hannie. "And I got nothing about the Troll Hunter's whereabouts."

"Uh-huh." Small nodded thoughtfully. "Well, we'll find the Troll Hunter eventually, and the money will come in handy. As for Hannie, we can't really risk taking her back right now. We could leave her here for them to find…" he said as Hannie wailed, "…but she might be useful again." Small watched Bog. "It's up to you."

"Please, Bog?" Hannie dropped to her knees, her hands clasped together. Her clothes were filthy. She stank like a human. But she'd helped more than once.

Bog heaved to his feet. Why had he saved her? Maybe it was a flaw he'd inherited from Jeddal and Kasha. After all, they'd tolerated him. Maybe they would have saved Hannie, too.

"We'll have to find a stream where you can wash," he said, finally.

"Oh, thank you, Bog!" Hannie gushed. "I'll never forget this. I—" She glanced at his face and abruptly stopped. "Sorry, I'll be quiet. Really, I will."

11

TROLL HUNTER

THEY waded through a river to cover their trail. Bog made Hannie wash off the human stink and rub her skin and clothes with leaves to dull her odour. Then they travelled south toward Thunder City for the rest of the night.

Their pace was grueling, but Small said they could reach the city's edge in about four nights, if they kept it up. After they defeated the Troll Hunter, the Sleeping Giant would be just east—apparently they'd be able to see his silhouette from the city.

Small led, relying on Frantsum's stories of the terrain. Hannie rode on Small's shoulders, ducking low-hanging branches and keeping her promise to be quiet—most of the time. Bog brought up the rear, pondering ways to crush the Troll Hunter, once they found him.

They walked parallel to a road that Small called a highway, keeping to the trees and bushes. The highway was wider than the dirt road through Bog's forest, and paved smooth like those in Strongarm. It was louder, too, with trucks and cars blistering by.

Bog's nose hurt more now that the fight was over. He couldn't catch a scent unless he blew the snot out and breathed in deeply. A jagged wound snaked across it, helping to make up for its puny size.

At daybreak, they found a cavern tucked into the rounded grey rocks on the edge of a glassy lake. As they settled for the day, Hannie let out a piercing howl.

Bog held his ears. "You promised you'd stay quiet."

"Thunder's gone." Hannie hunched over her pink rucksack, wailing.

Thunder? He glanced at the sky—cloudless with the hint of dawn above the treetops.

"It's her doll," Small said. He patted her back with a heavy hand.

Bog rolled his eyes. Her gaudy doll with the blue fur, jewel in its belly, and human clothes?

Hannie's tiny shoulders heaved. Tears hung from her chin and dripped onto her shirt. "I…must have…dropped her…in town." Her blubbering broadcast their location.

"Stop crying," Bog said louder than he meant to.

Hannie gulped and then began to sob quietly.

Small sat back on his heels, frowning.

Hannie's whimpering tugged at Bog. He knelt down in front of her. "My grandmother says…" he paused, thinking how he shouldn't share troll lore with Hannie, but it was better than listening to her sob. "She says that you can turn humans into trolls by rubbing them with magic ointment, stretching their arms, and howling into their ears."

"Really?" Hannie leaned forward.

Small nodded. "I've heard that, too."

"She says that after a few moons, you can't tell the humans from the trolls."

"Do you have the magic ointment, Bog?" Hannie's eyes were hopeful.

"Naw. Never have seen any. But I can show you how to yank and stretch your nose each morning before sleep. Kasha—my grandmother—does it for all the youngsters. It gives them noses to be proud of."

"She does?" Her eyebrows puckered.

"Sure. Just spit on your hand, since we have no ointment." Bog honked a slug-like gob onto his palm.

Hannie hesitated, wrinkling her nose. Then she imitated him. "Like this?"

"Yup." Her attempt was pathetic. "Then rub and pull like this." He yanked at his nose, even though it hurt, while Hannie tried to grip her ugly button nose.

"Will this make me a troll?" Hannie sniffled between rubs.

Bog hesitated, not wanting to lie.

Small looked at him sideways.

Hannie caught Small's glance. "It won't. It's only a story." Her voice was accusing.

"Uh…" Bog shrugged, not sure how to calm her.

Hannie's face collapsed into another sulky mess. She tucked her knees into her chest and stared off into the western shadows with a vacant expression, silent tears streaming.

Watching her, Bog wondered why he cared about her mood. Small hovered over Hannie, too, trying to amuse her with shape-shimmering stunts, but she wouldn't stop crying.

That day, they shared a den for the first time— with Small in the middle. Bog told himself that it was because the den was large and because Hannie didn't smell so bad anymore. He planned to make her wash every night.

At breakfast the next night, Hannie's chin still trembled. Every so often, a stray tear found a path down her cheek. Neither Small nor Bog could cheer her up. They started the night's walk with everyone brooding. The mournful cry of a loon echoed Hannie's sorrow. Bog found himself wishing for her babble like the rush of a stream over rocks.

They scooted around a town called Gull, and later,

a lone house with a sleeping collie. They stopped to tangle the collie's long fur into knots without even waking him—a prank that failed to lighten Hannie's mood—and to hunt for leopard frogs in a nearby pond. Bog caught almost as many frogs as Small did. He hoped Ruffan was having as much luck.

In a marsh as wide as it was long, Bog and Small left soggy footprints while Hannie rode on Small's shoulders. Rotten trees had uprooted in the water, and Bog picked up a gnarled piece of root, thinking of the figures that Jeddal had carved for him when Bog was a youngster. The root was about the size of his hand. Bog could see the shape of a troll with a crooked nose hiding within the wood.

While they walked, Bog whittled away at the root with his fingernail, slowly carving the soggy lump into a worthy imitation of a troll. Later, beside their cookfire, he was still at it.

At dinner, Bog crunched his own frogs whole, hardly savouring the meager but tasty meat. He carved after dinner, too, refusing to show Small his creation when he asked. Hannie sat beside the fire, staring into the flames with mournful eyes that tugged at him. She didn't even touch her roasted frogs.

Bit by bit, Bog whittled a face into the root, along with crude arms and legs. He knotted hair from cedar twigs and wedged in eyes of bone. When he was done, he shoved the doll at Hannie.

"Here."

Hannie glanced at the carving, her expression vacant. Then her face lightened, warming Bog from nose to tail.

"Oh," she whispered. "Is she for me?"

"It comes with a story." Bog shifted closer to the glowing embers in the firepit, telling himself the gift was to keep her useful. "So be quiet."

Small raised an eyebrow. Bog launched into his tale, before he could change his mind about telling it.

"I was too old for toys when my father, Jeddal, handed me a doll he'd carved himself, much like this one." Bog motioned toward Hannie's doll. "We'd just returned from a hunt with fresh muskrat for dinner."

Hannie's wide eyes reflected the firelight.

"'A doll?' I asked him," Bog continued. "My father nodded and said, 'And more. Look closer.' I examined the thing. Like yours, it was carved from root but had snail-shell eyes and a feathered tail."

"Oooh. I like feathers." Hannie edged closer.

"Then Jeddal said, 'A troll doll is never just a doll. It's a talisman, a story, a guide. The body of Ymir inhabits bone and stone, wood and earth. Remember to listen, Bog. The truth can be found in even a clump of moss.'" Bog leaned back against a rock and crossed his arms.

"What does that mean?" Hannie said.

Bog shrugged and thought for a moment. "Maybe it means that a doll can teach you how to be a troll."

"Bog! Do you think so?" Hannie wrapped her arms around his neck—until she remembered her promise not to touch him and backed off.

"Are you doubting my father?" A growl rumbled in Bog's chest.

"Never." Hannie hugged her doll, smiling.

From across the flames, Small nodded.

Bog didn't know who needed the story more—Hannie or himself.

The walking was endless. Sharp rocks jabbed Bog's feet. His legs throbbed with a dull pain that cool lake water couldn't soothe, although his nose was less swollen and he could smell again.

On the third night of travelling from Strongarm, Bog scented meat cooking. "Is it…hamburgers?" He didn't quite trust his nose. Hamburgers in the forest?

Small licked his lips. "Hamburgers would be nice."

"I see a light near the road," Hannie said. She was walking, for a change.

Small inhaled. "Humans. Maybe a restaurant?"

"A what?" Bog wouldn't mind hamburgers for dinner.

"Oooh. Let's go. Please, please, please, Small?" Hannie bounced on her toes, clutching her new doll. "I want to have a milkshake. And some French fries—I miss French fries. And some chocolate. Do you think they'll have chocolate?"

"Slow down." Small patted her on the head. "If it is a restaurant," he said to Bog, "we could try to find out more about the Troll Hunter's den."

"But what about—" Hannie began.

"Of course, we'd need to buy a few hamburgers, too." Small grinned. "We've got the money."

Hannie cheered.

"Is it safe?" Bog asked.

"It should be." Small scratched his chin. "Maybe you and Hannie could go together—ask about the Troll Hunter and order us some take-out."

"What is *take-out*?" Bog asked. "Is it better than hamburgers?"

"I know how to order food. I can show Bog what to do." Hannie yanked Small's hand. "Let's go. I'm sick of snakes and mice."

Bog traded a smile with Small. Some troll she was.

From his rucksack, Small fitted Bog with a long-sleeved shirt and a rounded hat with a brim that Hannie called a baseball cap. They were better than the raincoat and hat, although not by much. Bog still had to wear the hated black rain pants that crushed his tail, but he told himself it would be worth it if they found out more about the Troll Hunter's whereabouts. Soon, Bog and Hannie were heading toward the light of the restaurant, with Hannie chattering about how to order food and what she was going to eat first.

The restaurant faced the highway. Two cars sat out

front, silent and still. Blinding light spilled from the large windows onto scraggly bushes, forcing Bog to pull the cap down to shade his eyes. Peering through the windows, he counted one woman behind a long counter, leaning her chin on her hands, and a man eating alone at one of the many tables. The smell was stronger now—chicken, hamburgers, oil, and vegetables.

"Tell me again how we order?" Bog pulled Hannie back. Things hadn't gone so well the last time he'd entered a building.

"You ask about the Troll Hunter and I'll order. Okay, Bog? I'll ask for two hamburgers for you and Small, and then stuff for me."

"Four hamburgers—each."

"You can eat four hamburgers? Wow."

"Maybe you should get six for Small, just in case."

"If you say so. Do you have the money?"

Bog held out his fist with the crumpled paper money in it.

"Good. Let's go. I'm starving." Hannie marched up and flung open the door.

A bell on the door let out an ear-piercing jingle that made Bog's head ring, too. The woman behind the counter looked up as they entered. Bog stiffened. How should he greet her? Humans didn't pull noses.

The woman gave him a quick glance. "What'll you have?" she asked in the human tongue, ignoring Hannie.

"Uh…" All human words left him. "D-d-do you

know where the Troll Hunter is?" He stuttered.

"What? Only us folk here." She gestured vaguely.

The man who was eating alone studied Bog and Hannie.

"Yes, but…" Bog shifted his feet. "Do you know where the Troll Hunter's den is?"

The woman raised one eyebrow. "Sure, buddy. Just give me your order."

"Uh…" He ducked his head so his hat blocked her view of his face. "We w-want hamburgers," he said.

"Two hamburgers?" The woman scribbled on a pad of paper. Bog stared at the strange markings, wondering what they meant. "Do you want fries with that?"

Fries? He was relieved when Hannie pushed in front of him, climbing onto one of the stools that lined the counter.

"Yup. We'll have ten hamburgers, an order of fries, and a strawberry milkshake to go…do you have any white freezies?" She spun back and forth on the stool.

"Just ice cream." The woman scribbled more strange markings on the pad.

The man stared out the window.

Bog was glad to be ignored.

"But I wanted my friend to try a white freezie," Hannie whined. "Do you have any chocolate?"

"Over there." The woman pointed to a shelf of brightly packaged food that smelled too sweet. "Is that all?"

"Uh, yes. Except for the chocolate."

The woman ripped a paper off the pad and then called out, "Order." She handed the paper to a greasy-looking man who appeared at a window to a back room.

Bog heard the man slap the raw meat onto the heat. He smelled it cooking. His stomach grumbled. He squirmed in his clothes.

"Let's get some chocolate." Hannie tugged at his shirtsleeve.

Bog followed Hannie away from the counter. He didn't think the woman suspected he was a troll, although he was glad the clothes hid his tail and fur.

Near the shelf of chocolate, Bog was distracted by a glowing box mounted on the wall. It was just like the one in Hannie's house. He squinted into the flashing light. Was that a tiny human? Inside the box? He looked real enough, but he had no smell.

"That man is so small." Bog nudged Hannie. "How did he get in the box?" Maybe it was magic.

Hannie glanced up. "He's not in the box. It's just a picture on TV. Lots of humans watch TV. I used to like it, before I remembered that I'm a troll." She turned back to the rows of food on the shelf. "Do you like chocolate?"

The scent of the cooking meat made his mouth water. "I don't know." He watched as a new man appeared in the box.

"…we interrupt this program with another emergency news bulletin," the man said.

"Well, I like chocolate and I think you should try it. I don't know anyone who doesn't like chocolate so you have to like it," Hannie chattered.

"Police are continuing to track the fierce troll that attacked James Vincent and kidnapped his seven-year-old daughter, Hannie Vincent, in Strongarm three nights ago. They're rumoured to be heading for the Sleeping Giant," said the man in the box.

Bog froze. The man was talking about them. He was the fierce troll.

The man in the box continued. "Residents in the area have been warned to stay inside at night, with doors and windows locked. Any sightings should be reported to your local police station."

Bog glanced uneasily around the restaurant. The woman was busy with a machine on the counter, and the man eating alone was still ignoring them.

"The creature matches the description of a troll who recently attacked an illegal lumber camp near Strongarm, which police have since closed down." The scene in the box changed to show the barren hills where Bog once stood with Small.

Bog wasn't sure what *illegal* and *police* meant, but closed down—wait until Small heard.

The man appeared in the box again. "Here, again, is a sketch of the troll," he gestured at a black-and-white drawing of a troll with nicely pointed teeth and a wicked grin, "who is described as small but extremely cunning."

Bog stretched a little taller. The troll in the sketch

had a handsomely long nose.

"Earlier today, police called in Martinique Bottom—an expert Troll Hunter who recently settled in Thunder City—to trap this troll and rescue the girl."

Bog gasped. Martinique Bottom! His mother. No. It couldn't be. She wouldn't...hunt trolls?

The glowing box displayed a human female. Bog stepped back. His legs trembled. His mother was surprisingly pretty, with a longish nose, three welts along one cheek, and stringy grey hair down to her shoulders.

"Tune in at eleven for an exclusive interview with Troll Hunter Martinique Bottom, including a report of her time spent hunting the deadly western mountain troll—"

"Bog, I said, do you like caramel?" Hannie thumped the side of his leg.

"Your order's ready," said the woman behind the counter. "That'll be seventy-nine dollars and sixty cents. You want the chocolate, too?"

The smell of hamburgers sickened Bog. He gaped at the woman, unable to speak.

12

HUNTED

BOG had three hamburgers left in his paper bag. The size of the throbbing hollow in his gut. His mother was the Troll Hunter, chasing him down. How could he eat?

The moon rippled carelessly among the lily pads dotting the pond. Bog and Small hurried over deadwood and around patches of reeds, putting some distance between them and the restaurant. Hannie was perched on Small's shoulders, clinging to his fur as she tried to sip from a plastic cup through a tube she called a straw.

"It's great news that the logging camp is shut down, but I still can't believe the Troll Hunter is female!" Small shook his head and then glanced at Bog's bag of hamburgers. "Are you going to eat those?"

Without slowing his pace, Bog tossed the bag to

Small. It had been hard enough to choke down one hamburger, just so he'd have the strength to keep walking. His mother was willing to kill any troll she found. How could he be descended from a murderer? And what should he do now—hunt his own mother? Kill her? He shuddered.

Small unwrapped a hamburger. "So we know the Troll Hunter will try to trap us, probably try to turn us to stone. The question is: Do we set our own trap and let her come to us, or do we continue toward Thunder City, watching for her?" He shoved the useless bread back into the bag, along with the wrapping. "What do you think, Bog?"

Bog turned from the scent of hamburgers, disgusted. "Maybe we should go after the Nose Stone." If he didn't rescue Jeddal, Bog would never know the truth. Jeddal held the answers to so many questions—why Bog's mother was a troll hunter, why Jeddal had mated with her, who Bog was.

"With the Troll Hunter after us? Maybe we should cause some trouble to let the Troll Hunter know where we are. Then we can leave a trail to a trap." Small stuffed meat into his mouth.

Bog picked up his pace, as if he could outrun the idea. "No, it's too risky," he said. "We should get the Nose Stone and deal with her later."

Small frowned. "I owe you a *gnark*, so I'll follow where you need me to go. But why are you suddenly set on finding the Nose Stone when more trolls are being turned to stone every time the sun rises?"

"She's too dangerous," Bog said.

"Diama said the Troll Hunter can track a fish through water." Hannie shuddered. Then she reached down as far as she could, offering Bog some brown food the size of a twig. "Try some chocolate. You'll love it."

"No human food." Bog knocked her hand away, ignoring the hurt expression on her face and the sickly sweet scent of the chocolate. Even after Jeddal's warnings about humans, Bog had been foolish enough to reveal secrets to Hannie. He stepped over an aspen log that had been gnawed by a beaver.

"Please, Bog? Just one bite?" Hannie pleaded.

Bog shook his head, remembering Hannie yelling out to her father. *I'm going to the Sleeping Giant with Bog. And even after we find the Nose Stone, I'm not coming back.* Thanks to Hannie, the Troll Hunter knew where they were going and what they were after.

Small juggled the bag and the hamburgers, dropping crumbs and slowing their pace. Hannie slid sideways off his shoulders.

"Help," she squealed, gripping one side of Small's head while trying to hold her drink.

Small grabbed her with a furry hand. A hamburger bun dropped out of the bag.

"Be quiet, Hannie." Bog scowled. "Small, you're leaving a trail." He pointed to the bun.

"What does it matter? Would it be so bad if the

Troll Hunter found us?" Small worked Hannie's tiny fingers free from his left eye.

How could Bog explain without revealing his secret? He picked up the bun and shoved it in the bag. "If we want to outsmart the Troll Hunter and rescue Jeddal, we'll have to be wickedly cunning. No more cooking fires. No dropped buns. And we should get to the Sleeping Giant as fast as we can."

"It'll take two nights to get there. How can we go any faster?"

"Maybe we could travel by day, if we stick to the shadows," Bog said.

Small stopped to gape at him, his teeth caked with meat.

Bog avoided Small's gaze. "It's a stupid idea. I know. I'm just...let's get going. We can't stand around."

He took a few steps up the next ridge, raising his nose to catch the scent of owl scat and car fumes. When Bog sensed that Small wasn't following, he spun around.

Small's furry arms were folded across his chest. "What is it?"

"What are you talking about?" Bog tried to keep his voice calm.

"You won't eat. You want to travel in the sun. What's wrong with you?"

"What do you think is wrong?" Bog spoke too loud. "The Troll Hunter is tracking us."

"Let her come. She's only human. We'll outwit her,

and then we'll get the Nose Stone and restore your father."

What could Bog say to make Small understand? His mother had learned about trolls from Jeddal so she knew as much as he did. She'd lived with a troll. She'd mothered a troll. What if she could outmaneuver them?

"You're right." Bog frowned. "But I still want to get the Nose Stone first."

Small's eyebrows were a furry mound. He stared as if trying to understand. "I heard you, Bog. But there'll be no travelling by day, no matter where we're headed," he said. Then he hiked up the ridge, brushing by Bog.

Hannie twisted sideways on Small's shoulders. "Come on," she called.

Bog hurried after them, wishing he didn't have to keep secrets from his friend.

They walked as far as they could before the sun forced them to stop. Bog slept little that day, yelling out with horrible dreams of his mother blasting apart the den they'd dug for themselves, exposing them to the sun's harsh rays.

The next evening, the lights of Thunder City cast a disturbing glow across the sky, making the forest shadows gloomier. They marched toward the glow, watching for any signs of a trap. When the highway they'd been following south from Strongarm met a second highway, Small directed them east, parallel to this new highway, toward the Sleeping Giant.

Trucks and cars bellowed past, belching out fumes. The lights of Thunder City were behind them now, making Bog feel as if humans might sneak up on them.

"How many people do you think live there?" Bog gestured at the city's glow.

"I dunno." Small lumbered on. He was carrying Hannie on his shoulders again. "Maybe a thousand?"

"I've never seen that many trolls in one place." The idea of a city reminded Bog of a nest of ants. How horrible to live close to so many.

"Me neither. Seems awful crowded."

"I've been to Thunder City. It's huge—with more people than you can count," Hannie babbled. "My aunt used to live there, before she ran away to become a troll. She used to make chocolate chip cookies and yummy macaroni and cheese, and she always read me stories at night. Once she took me swimming and another time we went camping…"

Bog stopped listening, concentrating on smelling instead. Too many human scents. All around. He could smell the machinery they used to hack apart trees, make more roads, and destroy troll territory.

"According to my pa," Small said when Hannie had finished, "the lake and the Sleeping Giant should be just south of this highway."

They crossed the highway once the stream of trucks and cars slowed for the night. Bog ran over the stinking tar and stone, hating the heat of it under his feet. He burst into the cover of the forest on the other side, breathing fast, and climbed a steep slope covered in balsam and pine. Branches blocked out most of the night sky, shielding them from the city's glare. His legs shook, but he pushed on. Beside him, Small faltered on some loose rocks and then set Hannie down to make her own way up the slope.

At the top of the ridge, the trees thinned and a water-scented wind hit Bog's nostrils. He gasped. Beyond the last wrinkle of forest lay a vast body of water with no shore on the far side. Endless waves peaked in white crests, heaved, and then crashed back into the froth.

"Superior Lake." Small gaped at the view.

"That's a lake?" Bog inhaled deeply. "It must be an ocean." As big as Ymir's footprint.

"That's where my aunt took me to swim. It's really cold water." Hannie shivered.

Small pointed east to a long peninsula that stretched out against the purple-grey clouds.

"And there's the Sleeping Giant." He slapped Bog on the shoulder. "We made it."

The Sleeping Giant. In a lake as vast as a sea. The noble profile of his face was a silhouette against the night sky. He rested on his back, his feet extended into the lake.

The Sleeping Giant would spend an eternity as rock. Bog bowed his head and blinked back tears. The giant would want no one's pity.

Later that night, as they hiked across yet another valley, Bog scented troll. More than one. He stopped abruptly.

Small sniffed the air. "I smell them, too." He lowered Hannie from his shoulders.

"Smell what?" Hannie gripped his hand.

"Shh," they both said.

Hannie inhaled. "Aha," she whispered uncertainly. "I smell them."

Bog ignored her. His muscles were tense, ready to fight.

They edged forward, smelling frantically. When Bog tipped his nose high, he was rewarded with a new scent. Human—maybe from the night before. The sharp odour burned his nostrils and made him feel strangely sick to his stomach. For a moment, he could hear someone singing, soft and low.

A scent-memory? Bog shook his head to clear it. "Do you smell—"

"Yes," Small whispered.

"What?" Hannie tugged Small's fur.

Then they saw it. In a clearing surrounded by pine trees. A whole family of forest trolls turned to stone.

Bog fell to his knees. "No!"

Hannie let out a wail and ran to the trolls. "What happened?"

Bog shook his head, stunned. If it had been a trap, it had worked too well.

Two youngsters, a large male, and a smaller female. The statues were fresh—not worn by rain—and they still emitted a faint scent of troll. Worst of all, each statue had been broken—a nose, an ear, or a hand snapped off—and stone body parts lay in the pine needles at their feet.

The Nose Stone could never revive them.

Bog struggled to his feet. A tremor began in his thighs and spread until even his teeth were chattering. These statues were a message. Some human had broken them on purpose—Bog could smell the human's fading scent. A human who knew about the legend of the Nose Stone.

Then Bog smelled another troll approaching, behind them, moving through the bushes.

Before Bog could react, Small jumped between him and the rustling leaves.

"Let me handle it," Small whispered.

The branches swayed. Small lunged into the undergrowth.

Hannie shrieked.

Small dragged out a puny forest troll with a feathery tail who looked older than Ruffan but twice as scrawny.

"I'm a friend! A friend!" The troll bellowed. "My name is Hornel."

Small wrestled him to the ground and sat on his chest. Hornel struggled uselessly.

"Let him up," Bog said, feeling sorry for Hornel. "He doesn't look like a threat." With his tiny nose, Hornel was a pathetic troll.

Small studied the troll. "I guess you're right." He got off Hornel and then helped him up.

"Sorry, friend," Small said.

Hornel looked ready to cry. Bog offered him a swig of water.

"What happened here?" Bog asked gently. This troll might be a brand-new orphan.

"I…can't talk yet," Hornel whimpered. "I need a mouse…to…to soothe my stomach."

Bog and Small exchanged a look.

After they caught a mouse and Hornel devoured it, he began to speak. "The Troll Hunter did it." Hornel's hands trembled and his eyes darted back and forth. "She took my whole family."

Bog swallowed hard. That sharp odour *had* held a scent-memory. His mother had done this to innocent trolls.

"She's been attacking trolls in the area, trying to find the cave troll who kidnapped a human girl." Hornel looked pointedly at Hannie and then Bog. "She thinks you're searching for the Nose Stone."

"What do you know about the Nose Stone?" Bog tried to keep his voice calm, even though his insides boiled like white water.

"There's a local story. Everyone around here knows it. But the Troll Hunter only knew that you were looking for the Nose Stone, until she forced Pa to tell her what it is. That's why she came after us…for the story…" He sobbed, picked up an ear-shaped rock, and tried to fix it back on the largest stone troll— likely his father. "She's evil. If you'd seen her, you'd know. She enjoyed turning them to stone, and she'll do it again. I only survived because I hid from her."

"I'm sorry." Bog wondered what other horrors his mother was capable of. "She probably set a trap for us, and now your family…"

The troll wiped his eyes. "It's not your fault. Everyone knows you're a hero."

"A hero?" Bog shook his head.

Hannie cheered. "I knew he was."

"You destroyed a logging camp and stole a human right from her den." Hornel gave Hannie a cautious sniff. "But what I don't understand is, why did you kidnap her?"

"They didn't kidnap me," Hannie said. "I'm a troll."

Hornel glanced from Bog to Small.

Small shrugged.

Bog leaned close to Hornel, whispering, "She's been…useful." Most of the time.

"Like a guide?"

"Not really. More like—"

"A spy," Small interrupted. "She tells us human secrets."

As long as she didn't share any more troll secrets. "Tell me about the Nose Stone," Bog said to Hornel, who was studying Hannie warily. "Is it real? Why hasn't anyone found it?"

"Of course it's real. It's just impossible to get to. It's hidden underground on an island. Silver Island, it's called." He pointed toward Superior Lake. "That's where the Troll Hunter went. She wants to destroy the Nose Stone."

Bog's jaw tightened. If he didn't find the Nose Stone first, Jeddal could be stone forever. Why had he waited so long to go after it? "What do you mean *impossible to get to*?"

Hornel glanced nervously at the scrub bushes as if he expected the Troll Hunter to leap out of them at any moment. "Some humans built a wall around the island with tunnels down into the rock to mine the silver. They took most of the silver, before the mine shafts were destroyed by the lake. At least, that's what my pa told her."

"Just like Frantsum said." Small nodded.

Bog tried to stay calm. "Did your pa ever mention a secret entrance?"

"Yes. But he didn't tell the Troll Hunter about it."

"Good," Bog said. "Did he know where the entrance is?"

"Pa said it was on the highest peak around the bay. That one, over there." Hornel pointed to a hill farther east, his hand still shaking. "He said the entrance looks like a stone with three mouths. He spent a lot of time on that hill, searching for it. But he never found it."

Small's face fell. Bog's muscles tightened. Maybe they were chasing a phantom.

"Thanks, Hornel." Bog patted him on the shoulder, more gently than Small would have. "You're a cunning troll and a good friend. Do you have a den to go to? Any family nearby?"

"No." Hornel's chin trembled. "But I'm old enough to take care of myself."

"Then I want you to leave here. Go far away, where the Troll Hunter won't find you. I don't want any more stonings." Bog's nostrils flared, taking in his mother's scent.

"Or I could go with you. I'd be a good guide," Hornel pleaded.

"It's too risky. I need to know you're safe."

"But I know the way to—"

"We'll be fine." Bog swished his tail.

"All right." Hornel's shoulders slumped. "Good luck, Bog. May Ymir's eye shine on you. I hope you find the Nose Stone and kill the Troll Hunter."

Bog stiffened. Was there no other way to stop his mother?

"Those are harsh words for a troll," Small said.

Hornel gestured toward his family, his eyes misting. "A monster like her doesn't deserve to live."

"I suppose." Small nodded grimly.

Hornel yanked noses with them, although he refused to go near Hannie, who pouted. He lingered over his family, touching his stubby nose against each one. Then he scuttled away.

"I want you to leave, too," Bog told Small. "Take Hannie with you."

"No." Small's eyes glinted in the moonlight.

"I can't be responsible for any more stonings. If the Troll Hunter finds us…" Bog's throat tightened.

"I can't leave you." Small put a hand on Bog's shoulder. "I want to see this through."

Bog turned from the fierce glow on Small's face. Would Small still help if he knew Bog's secret?

"I'm not leaving either." Hannie stomped her foot. "I can help. I'm good at lots of things."

"Fine." Bog nodded. "Let's find the Nose Stone before the Troll Hunter destroys it."

13

THE GIANT'S SECRET

THEY hurried to a forest-covered hill on the shoreline, just west of the peninsula that was the Sleeping Giant. The smell of humans on the breeze made Bog jittery.

"Is this the highest point in the bay?" He peered at the silhouette of land against the glow of scattered starlight.

"I can't tell." Small pushed back the branches of a balsam fir for a better view.

They were close enough to the Sleeping Giant that his shape was too massive to take in.

"I think it's higher over there." Hannie pointed to the tree-topped cliffs that formed the western side of the Sleeping Giant.

"The entrance to the mine can't be on the Sleeping Giant." Bog frowned at Hannie. "When the humans hid the Nose Stone, he wasn't stone."

"Maybe he's lying on top of it." Hannie grabbed his tail to steady herself on a wobbly rock. "That's why no one can find it."

Bog jerked his tail free. "Where was the highest point of land before the Sleeping Giant was turned to stone?" He said to Small.

"From here, this hill looks the highest," Small said.

"Agreed." Bog nodded grimly. "Let's search."

They organized into a row an arm's-length apart and then hiked from the top of the hill toward the water, searching for the stone with three mouths.

Bog tried not to get discouraged when they reached the waves lapping against the shore.

"Let's move east and try again." He growled.

They scurried back up the hill, scanning for any sign of the entrance. Human voices echoed across the bay. Was his mother on the Sleeping Giant right now, looking for the Nose Stone?

Over and over, they traipsed in parallel tracks up and down the hill, moving slowly eastward. They pushed through prickly shrubs, stepped in moose droppings to disguise their scents, and examined rocks coated with lichen. Nowhere did they find a stone with three mouths.

When the hillside finally sloped into a ravine, they fell, exhausted, against a moss-covered log.

"Ymir, where is it?" Bog whispered to the moon.

"We'll find it." Small thumped his back.

Bog stiffened, letting the pain of the blow flower and then die away.

"I'm tired." Hannie sighed. "My legs hurt. Can we eat now?"

"Not yet." Bog got to his feet. "We need to keep searching."

"I don't know, Bog. Soon we'll have to stop for the day." Small lurched upright, startling a nearby flying squirrel, which glided away with limbs spread.

Bog scowled at the eastern sky, which was just starting to lighten.

They ventured onto the Sleeping Giant to find shelter. Although Bog doubted that the tunnel entrance could be found among the cliffs, he couldn't help searching as they went for the stone with three mouths.

On the western side of the Sleeping Giant, they found a cliffside cave with a majestic view of the lake. Reluctantly, Bog agreed to stop. Red-orange sunlight dominated the eastern sky.

They caught a few deer mice for dinner, which Hannie refused to eat unless they were cooked. Small insisted they could risk a tiny fire, since they were isolated. Bog wondered if they should chance it.

Once the fire had been stamped out, Bog sat alone at the mouth of the cave, contemplating the purple shroud of the western sky. A white-throated sparrow sang on a nearby branch, welcoming the morning sun. Bog growled at it, startling the bird into flight.

He couldn't stop worrying that they'd never find the entrance to the mine.

What if the Nose Stone was just a story? What if the Sleeping Giant never had it?

What if Bog's mother destroyed it?

He might never get Jeddal back. He might be left with a mother who hunted trolls.

The sky lightened to a pale grey-blue, but Bog wasn't sleepy. He retreated farther into the cave, where Small lay propped against a sloping rock. Hannie was curled in his lap with her troll doll tucked under her chin, already asleep.

"We should talk," Bog said.

"We should sleep." Small yawned and shut his eyes. His furry arms were draped around Hannie.

"Just listen." Bog thumped Small hard enough to keep him awake. "We've searched everywhere on that hill for the entrance. Maybe it's not there. Hornel's story could be wrong."

Small nodded sleepily.

"I know the mine tunnels were flooded long ago, but maybe we should search for the Nose Stone on Silver Island."

"Yeah, that makes sense." Small tilted his head to one side. "We could also take care of the Troll Hunter, while we're there. Hornel said she's on the island."

"No," Bog said quickly. "I think we should avoid the Troll Hunter, if we can. She's really clever. We might need more help to defeat her."

Small snorted. "Why? Humans aren't so smart."

"That's what Jeddal said. But Hannie's not dumb. And the Troll Hunter is supposed to be smarter than most humans. She's managed to do enough damage anyway. She might know more about trolls than we expect." If only he could tell Small the whole story.

"You think humans are just pretending to be dumb?" Small asked.

"Maybe. But this Troll Hunter is cunning. You know she'll be setting traps for us—maybe guarding the way into the mine." Bog couldn't forgive himself if something happened to Small or Hannie.

"Yeah." Small's bronze eyes glimmered. "She wants Hannie back, and she wants to stone us."

Bog nodded. "We have to be smart. Get the Nose Stone and get out. We can deal with her later, when the Nose Stone is safe."

"You could be right." Small stretched and then settled back against the rock.

Bog stared at the purple sky outside the cave, willing the darkness to return. "We'll start for the island at nightfall."

Bog woke to a storm brewing over the lake. Thunderous grey clouds mushroomed toward the Sleeping Giant. Waves ran before the storm-front, swelling until their edges were torn white.

They turned inland, away from the wind that

ripped at their fur and hair. Bog sniffed the air for his mother's scent—the sharp, biting smell that had penetrated his flesh like a wound.

They hiked farther south, heading for Silver Island at the feet of the Sleeping Giant. When the rain began, it chased the animals into their dens. Bog sloshed through muddy leaf scatter, soaking wet and shivering.

They avoided the few humans huddled under tarps and poking at the remains of campfires. Most often, the humans were snoring inside brightly coloured tents.

Near the end of the night, the rain stopped, although the trees continued to drip. They climbed down the Sleeping Giant's feet to the flat tip of the peninsula and skirted a few houses huddled among the trees near the lake. Bog felt as if someone were following him, or watching him. As they slipped past one building, his mother's sharp scent scorched his nostrils and carved into his memory, bringing up the sound of his mother singing, a cold wind rustling the leaves above him, the nauseating smell of roasting vegetables.

"She's been here," he said, banishing the scent-memory from his head.

Small tipped his furry nose high. "Uh-huh. Passed this way a while ago."

Bog inhaled again, trying to pinpoint her trail.

"Is it her? The Troll Hunter?" Hannie gripped Small's hand.

Small nodded, placing a finger over her mouth.

"She went that way." Bog pointed toward one of the houses. "Maybe she's asleep inside." He shuddered.

The sky was just starting to lighten. Bog wanted to get to the water's edge, maybe even find a way onto the island before they needed to find shelter.

They continued toward the water, avoiding a road that snaked between the houses. The trees and undergrowth hid them, although the rock-encrusted ground made sneaking difficult for Hannie.

"Careful!" Bog scolded her when she slipped, trapping her foot in a hollow under a large boulder.

As Small pulled Hannie free, the wind shifted. Bog smelled the sharp, biting scent again. Blood pounded in his ears as he refused a new scent-memory.

"Get down," he whispered, but Small was already yanking Hannie behind the bush where Bog squatted.

A human with bushy hair stood about three hundred paces away on a wooden landing that extended into the lake. Bog choked in a breath. His mother. In the flesh. What should he do?

Out on the water, lights shone like twinkling stars, bobbing on the waves, moving closer. A buzzing sound grew louder.

"Is that a—" he began.

The boat roared louder than a car. Bog and Small covered their ears until the roaring stopped, leaving the boat drifting toward the landing. One human sat in the boat.

"Noisy human," Bog hissed. His ears were still ringing.

Small nodded, rubbing his ears.

"What?" Hannie hadn't covered her ears at all.

"Be quiet," Bog whispered.

"Any luck?" A husky female voice called from the landing as the boat neared. His mother's voice. A wave of nausea rolled through Bog.

"Naw." A man's voice echoed over the water from the boat. "The diver can't get into most of the old mining tunnels. They're filled with rubble and the cribbing's destroyed. Maybe if you could be more specific about what he's looking for...but a rock shaped like a nose?" He shook his head. "Impossible."

"What'd he say?" Hannie crawled onto Small's shoulders.

Bog clenched his jaw. "They're searching for the Nose Stone."

"Over on Silver Island," Small added.

"Oh!" Hannie's grey eyes grew wide.

"...and I need you to keep searching," Bog's mother said. "It has to be somewhere on that island."

Bog whispered to Small. "We have to find the Nose Stone first."

A rustling noise came from behind them.

"What's that?" Bog hissed. Were humans closing in from downwind, surrounding them?

Small set Hannie down and got ready to pounce. Bog raised a fist to pound whoever came through the bushes.

Hornel emerged from the undergrowth, with his pathetic nose and scrawny body. "Did you kill the Troll Hunter yet?" he asked loudly, his voice carrying through the bushes toward the lake.

Small shushed him. Bog stiffened.

His mother's head swiveled toward the bushes where they crouched. "Did you hear that?" she asked the man.

Bog glared at Hornel, who shrank away from him.

"It could just be Larry," said the man.

"I'd better check it out." Bog's mother headed toward them. "We may have visitors."

Bog couldn't breathe.

Small was up first. "Run," he whispered, scooping Hannie into his arms and then hurtling farther into the undergrowth, back the way they'd come.

Bog raced after Small, dragging Hornel with him.

They got halfway between the houses and the lake, in the deepest part of the brush, when the ringing of a bell slammed through Bog's head. He stifled a scream.

Hornel curled into a ball.

Small dropped Hannie and grabbed his ears.

Bog stumbled away from the sound, his fingers shoved deep into his ears. He tripped and spun sideways to glimpse his mother moving through the trees, swinging a large handbell back and forth.

The same tactic as the puny man with the noise box.

Bog's hands itched to get at her, claw her, stop her, punish her for what she'd done to Jeddal and so many other trolls.

The ringing stopped.

Bog released his ears.

His head still pounded, his ears throbbed. He could sense his mother walking away from them now, farther west. He shadow-slipped behind a tree with Hornel, who shook like a leaf in a storm.

"What were you thinking?" Bog whispered. "I sent you away to keep you safe, to keep us all safe." His fingernails dug into his palms.

"I'm sorry. I didn't mean to…" Hornel grimaced. "I just wanted to help. I was lonely. I couldn't sit there and do nothing."

"So you followed us?"

"No. Since you were looking for the Nose Stone, I came after the Troll Hunter. When I smelled your scent, I—"

"Where's Hannie?" Small stumbled toward them.

A twig cracked nearby.

"I'm down here!" came a faint voice.

Hannie had slid into the hollow under the boulder where her foot had been trapped. As she tried to climb out, pine needles and leaves gave way at the hollow's edge. She slipped farther underground, her fingers scrabbling for a hold.

"Get me out!" Hannie whimpered softly.

Small tried to lift the boulder out of the way, but it wouldn't budge.

Bog glanced around, searching for his mother, who was nowhere in sight. Then he joined Small, struggling to lift the boulder free. Hornel just watched them, gripping his tail in his hands, his nose drooping.

Small grunted as they managed to slide the boulder away to reveal more than just a hollow. Bog gaped at the wide stone entrance to an underground cavern—an entrance with three wide openings and jagged rocks like teeth enclosing the middle mouth where Hannie still struggled to climb out.

"The tunnel!" Bog pointed. It had to be.

Hornel gasped. "You found it! Out here. But I thought…I can't believe it."

Small lifted Hannie out with one arm, his tail extended for balance. "Bog, this human is a good-luck charm."

Hannie clasped onto Small. "Did I do a good job, Small? Did I? 'Cause I try to. I really do."

"Who's there?" Bog's mother called in human talk, just as Bog caught her scent on the breeze. "Is that you, Larry?"

Bog's fur stood on end.

A panicked look crossed Hornel's face. "This is my fault." He pushed Bog toward the tunnel. "Go find the Nose Stone. I'll throw her off your track."

"No," Bog whispered. "It's too dangerous. Stay with us so we can—"

"That's the tunnel?" Hannie asked.

"Quiet," Bog and Small both said.

"I have to do this," whispered Hornel. "May Ymir guide you." He disappeared into the undergrowth.

A shiver crawled up Bog's spine, settling in his shoulders. "And you."

Bog prayed to Ymir that Hornel wouldn't end up like his family. Then he dove into the cavern, with Small and Hannie scrambling after him.

14

THE TUNNEL

WITH hands outstretched, Bog made his way deeper underground. He could hear Hornel pushing noisily away through the undergrowth outside the cavern, the rustling and footsteps growing fainter.

Bog flicked his tail. They'd escaped—for now. But would Hornel?

"He fooled the Troll Hunter once," Small whispered, as if he'd read Bog's mind. "He can do it again."

"I just wished he'd gone home or somewhere else that's safe. Why does he have to act the hero?"

"For the same reason you do?" Small said.

The fur on Bog's back prickled. Maybe scrawny Hornel had something to prove, too.

The cavern was cool, moist, and soothingly dark.

Once Bog's eyes adjusted, he could see a cave spider with long arched legs suspended in midair. He felt millipedes scurrying past his feet. A breeze gusted from the opening toward the back of the cavern. A good sign.

Bog followed the breeze, hoping it would show them the way through the rock. With Small's bulk, the space was cramped. Hannie was surprisingly quiet—maybe she finally understood the danger.

The cavern lengthened into a tunnel, leading deeper underground. Bog sniffed the breeze for the departing scent of Hornel and his mother. They were even farther off now.

His bristled fur relaxed. Maybe Hornel could escape the Troll Hunter. Maybe this darkness would lead to the Nose Stone.

The tunnel grabbed the wind from outside and twisted it into tiny whirlpools before thrusting it farther underground. Only Hannie was having trouble negotiating the uneven rock. He heard her stumbling, and even grunting.

"I can't see," she whispered. "Where are you, Small?"

Bog sensed Small turning sideways and then heard the swish of his tail.

"Grab on," Small said.

"Where?" Hannie struck some body part against rock.

More swishing.

"Got it."

"Good. Now hold on."

When Bog could no longer see much, he felt in his rucksack for a candle and then used Jeddal's flint stone to light it. He held the candle in front, sheltering it from the wind with his chest. Centipedes darted away from the light. Cave beetles scuttled into shadowy crevices.

The tunnel became a steep natural stairway of rock enclosed between narrow walls that just fit Small. The roof was low, too, so Small hunched over, scooping up bugs to snack on as he went.

"The Sleeping Giant would never have made it through here," Small whispered.

They crept forward. Bog could smell water nearby—and hear it trickling through rock. When he began to doubt the tunnel would lead anywhere, the candle lit up a stone archway.

"Look!" His voice bounced off the curved rock.

He stepped through the archway, holding the candle high. An underground chamber sparkled with an eerie light. Streaks and pinpricks of light speckled the walls.

"Oh!" Small gasped.

"Where's the light coming from?" Hannie asked, her voice pitched high.

"It's silver," Bog said, "reflecting the candlelight."

Wiry veins of silver ore snaked everywhere, catching the light in intricate patterns. It had been chipped away in places, perhaps by the Sleeping Giant's human partners. Farther in, the cave floor was flooded with water. A small underground stream sloshed and gurgled through the cavern and probably to the lake beyond.

"Sounds like Small's stomach after he eats." Hannie giggled.

"Do you see the Nose Stone?" Bog scanned for it. They had to find it. Jeddal's life depended on it.

"No. Let's go farther in," Small said.

They plunged into the cold water, which slowed them down, tugging at Bog's legs.

Toward the far end of the cavern stood a rough stone pillar about waist high for Bog and thigh high for Small.

Hannie's eyes widened. "Is that what you're looking for?"

Bog waded closer. Could it be? *Please, Ymir, let us find it.*

Silver lumps were arranged in a circle on the flat top of the pillar. Bog moved the candle closer, and the light reflected off the lumps.

Only then did he see it. In the centre of the circle—a place of honour. A plain grey stone.

Bog sucked in a breath.

"I can't believe it." Small shook his head.

"Let me see." Hannie splashed beside them.

Small hoisted Hannie, holding her under her armpits. She gasped. "Is that the Nose Stone?"

"I think so." Bog glanced at Small, who beamed. Could they really bring Jeddal back to life? He trembled, imagining the moment.

Hannie leaned forward. "Can I touch it?" She reached out a hand.

"No." Bog slapped her hand away. His voice echoed through the cavern, startling Small, who lost his grip on Hannie, dropping her in the water.

Hannie squealed, splashing and spluttering.

"Sorry. You all right?" Small hoisted her out of the water, dripping.

Hannie climbed up Small's chest by grabbing onto his fur. She settled on his shoulders and frowned at Bog. "What did you do that for?"

His stomached knotted. "The Nose Stone. It's special. You shouldn't touch it." It had been in the hands of humans for too long.

"Why not? I found this place."

Small nodded. "She's right."

"Yes, but…" She wasn't worthy.

Then Bog realized he didn't deserve to touch the Nose Stone either.

Silence fell over the cavern, except for the gurgle of the stream.

"Should we…take it?" Small finally asked.

"You get it," Bog said. Small was a full troll.

"No," Small said. "You do it. For Jeddal."

For Jeddal.

Bog nodded, grateful for his friend. Then he reached for the Nose Stone, lifting it with both hands.

The Nose Stone was as big as Bog's hand with his fingers extended. It was cold. Heavier than he expected. Mottled with shades of grey and flecks of off-white. One side was rounded and mostly smooth with a few warts, while the other was bumpy where it had broken off.

A tingle ran through Bog. He could almost feel the pulse of Ymir's blood in the rock, his magic seeking a home. He held Jeddal's chance for life in his hand.

On the pillar, where the Nose Stone had rested, a simple image had been carved into the rock. One large figure, perhaps the Sleeping Giant, reached out to a smaller tailless one, maybe a human. The carving was only a few lines, but it was enough for Bog to be sure this was the Nose Stone.

His skin warmed.

He could return to the clearing where Jeddal stood. He could free him from stone. He could help other trolls who'd been turned to stone.

Bog might be half human, but he could make up for what humans had done to trolls.

Small picked up the largest silver lump and gave it to Hannie. "For finding this place." He grinned. "It's time to start your own hoard."

Hannie gaped. "Oh, Small! I'll keep it forever. Bog, look. See how it sparkles? It's so pretty."

Both Bog and Small smiled. Small packed his rucksack with silver ore. Bog wrapped the Nose Stone in a cloth to keep it from chipping and then placed it at the bottom of his rucksack.

With Hannie admiring her lump of silver ore, they waded back the way they'd come. Bog and Small shook the water from their fur. They headed up the tunnel toward the entrance, leaving wet footprints behind them. With the Nose Stone in his rucksack, Bog felt as if he could tackle anything.

When they emerged from the tunnel, Bog hesitated. He saw no sign of his mother or Hornel—who had better be tucked into a makeshift den. The clouds had cleared. The sun was rising over the tips of the trees on the low eastern side of the Sleeping Giant. The distant settlement was quiet. Waves crashed on the shore of Superior Lake. Morning songbirds twittered.

Hannie squinted and yawned, shivering in her wet clothes.

"We need shelter fast. Maybe we should sleep there?" Bog jerked his head back at the tunnel.

Small studied the brightening sky and the shadows that still gathered under the trees. "I'd rather put some distance between us and the Troll Hunter. That opening is too exposed now."

"Agreed."

They shadow-slipped through the bushes and ferns, skirting a clearing where the first shafts of sunlight chased the darkness away.

"I saw a place earlier that should be large enough." Bog shielded his eyes from the too-bright beams. "Hurry."

He startled when he saw a figure standing ten paces away, on the edge of the clearing. Then he realized it was Hornel.

"Hornel! You're all right." Bog headed toward

him—until his mother's sharp odour sent a surge of horror through him.

He couldn't swallow. He couldn't exhale. Her scent evoked a new memory of a warm hearth made of bricks, dancing firelight, his father's deep laughter mixing with his mother's.

He shook his head, refusing to remember.

"I've been waiting for you."

He heard her gravelly voice, speaking in troll.

She stepped out from behind Hornel. The Troll Hunter. Martinique Bottom. His mother.

He glared at Hornel—at the weak wobble of his nose.

"I'm sorry." Hornel hung his head. "I tried. Really, I did."

15

DAWN

BOG'S mother stood at the edge of the clearing in the first brutal rays of sunlight. Her hands were planted on her hips. Her scraggly hair glowed like white fire. Insects buzzed through the beams of sunlight and danced across the clearing to the shadows where Bog clustered with Small and Hannie.

Bog sniffed the breeze for other humans or trolls, his muscles taut. Just Hornel—the useless one— huddled in front of Bog's mother in the shade of a fir tree.

Bog's fur stood on end. Did his mother know who he was? Would she tell Small? He flicked his tail, his nostrils flaring. He didn't want to fight his mother, but he couldn't let her hurt anyone else.

"Get the girl," his mother ordered Hornel, speaking

in troll language.

Hannie yelped and hid behind Small, who let out a warning snarl.

"No!" Bog yelled, his chest suddenly too tight.

"She promised to let us go, if we give up the girl," Hornel whined.

Small growled. "And you believed her?"

Bog's head spun. A few moons ago, he'd have thought it a proper trade, but now…how could he trust his mother to care for Hannie? How could he trust her to let them escape? "The girl stays with us." He glanced at Small, who nodded.

Hornel eyed the sun and Bog's mother, his feathery tail shaking. "We have no choice!"

Bog scowled. "This isn't the way, Hornel."

"Well, I say it is!" Hornel dashed forward.

Bog lunged for him, but Hornel was agile for a weak-nosed troll. He darted between Small's arms, dodging his deadly fingernails.

Hannie shrieked.

Hornel gripped her by the middle and tugged her toward the clearing.

"Don't let him take me!" She thrashed.

Bog and Small sprang after them as Hornel pushed Hannie toward Bog's mother.

"I can't!" Hannie cowered as if the sun's rays could hurt her.

Bog's mother reached into the shadows and yanked both Hornel and Hannie into the sunshine.

"No!" Hornel raised his hand.

Hannie screamed, skidding along the rocky ground.

Breathing hard, Bog and Small halted at the edge of the clearing, their toes on the jagged line between shade and sun.

A crackling sound came from Hornel.

Bog gasped.

Small growled.

Then Hornel was stone, his eyes scrunched shut, his body crouched—every horrible detail perfectly preserved.

Just like Jeddal.

"That's better." Bog's mother grimaced, as if the sight of the statue sickened her.

"How could you?" Bog roared. Small howled in outrage. Hornel was reckless and naïve, but he hadn't earned this fate.

Bog's mother gripped Hannie by the arm and pulled her upright. Hannie hollered and kicked, but his mother wrapped one arm around Hannie's chest.

"Don't worry," she said to Hannie in human talk. "I'll get you back to Strongarm."

Hannie's eyes became hollow, black pits. "Please," she whispered. "Don't take me back there."

"Let her go." Bog couldn't bear the look in Hannie's eyes. He rocked back and forth, wishing he could dive into the sun to rescue her. No one deserved a father like Hannie's.

Bog's mother ignored him, struggling to keep hold of Hannie with one hand. She snapped off several of Hornel's fingers, tossing them to land in the leaf litter at Bog's feet.

"A remembrance of your friend. You're next." She retreated farther into the clearing, taking Hannie with her.

"Never." Bog growled.

A smug half-smile played across his mother's face. "I only need to hold you here a few minutes longer. The sun will do my work for me. Unless you want to run off and leave Miss Hannie Vincent? Why do you want her so badly?"

"I'm a troll. I belong with them. Let me go," Hannie whimpered. She pulled free but his mother grabbed her by the upper arm.

"They brainwashed you?" Bog's mother frowned. "Don't worry. I know people who can help." Then to Bog and Small, she said, "Now, hand over your sacks."

"Why?" Bog gripped the strap of his rucksack. He didn't dare look at Small, praying that Ymir would somehow protect their treasure.

His mother's eyes were beady. "I know you came here searching for the Nose Stone. Did you find it?"

"We found a cave," Bog held out his empty hands, "but no Nose Stone."

He wouldn't let Jeddal down. Maybe he could shape-shimmer the Nose Stone to keep it safe, but that wouldn't help for long. He could think of only one way to stop her, and it sickened him.

"I never trust a troll." His mother scowled. "Give

me your sacks—slowly, one at a time. I'll check for myself."

With a warning glance at Small's pinched face, Bog slid his rucksack off his shoulder and held it out toward her.

"Toss it at my feet." His mother edged forward warily, avoiding Hornel and dragging Hannie along beside her.

Bog calculated the distance left between them and devised a plan. He'd dive into the sun, trapping her under his bulk as he turned to stone. Small could hide Hannie somewhere safe, and then return at night to revive him with the Nose Stone. If his statue didn't crack. If the Nose Stone worked its magic.

Bog dropped his rucksack beside Hornel's severed stone fingers. Then he dove into the sun at his mother.

16

INTO THE SUN

SMALL yelled as Bog sailed through the air.

Hannie wailed.

His mother's eyes widened. She pushed Hannie to the side.

Bog thudded into his mother, knocking her to the ground, cheek to stinking cheek.

He squeezed his eyes shut, waiting for his heart, his blood, his flesh and bone to turn to solid rock.

This was it. He'd join Jeddal as stone.

"No!" Hannie screamed.

Could stone hear?

He took a breath. The air was warm in his lungs. His mother's stench was worse up close.

He opened his eyes to blinding brilliance, like a thousand piercing pine needles. He squinted, eyes watering. He couldn't see, but he could feel his mother squirming under him.

How was he still flesh and blood? Sunbeams beat down on his back, legs, arms, head.

His mother pushed him off. Veins throbbed at her temples.

He scrambled away from her and rose to his feet.

From the shadows, Small gaped.

Hannie raced to Bog and clamped on. "You're okay! Oh, I thought…" Then, for once, Hannie was speechless. She buried her face in his grey chest fur and sobbed.

"What *are* you?" his mother asked.

But Bog couldn't tear his eyes away from Small's face. Tawny fur framed the dropped-open circle of his mouth. His eyebrows were wooly mountains high on his forehead.

Small shook his head and backed up several paces.

Bog's cheeks burned.

The sun warmed his fur, his hide.

His diluted blood forced him to live.

He was a hopeless failure of a troll.

"Impossible," his mother was saying. "No troll can resist the sun. Tell me how you did it."

Bog ignored her. "I'm sorry, Small." How could he explain, after keeping the secret for so long? He tucked his tail between his legs. His eyes filled with tears.

Hannie wormed her fingers into his fur as she wrapped her arms around his shoulders.

Small's mouth closed into a tight line. His nose grew rigid.

"I tried to…" Bog began again, struggling to find a way to help Small understand. Then he blurted, "She's my mother." He pointed at her. "I'm half human. I…I couldn't tell you." He hid his face in Hannie's forest-scented hair, unable to watch Small's reaction. "Forgive me."

A heavy silence fell over the clearing.

Bog squeezed Hannie.

"What?" She squirmed free of his arms. "You're what?"

"It can't be." He heard the disbelief in his mother's voice. "He said you were dead."

He turned to his mother, who was circling behind him, as if trying to see him from all angles.

"Patrick?" she whispered.

That name. He'd heard it before. The memory came like a slap to the face—his mother sing-songing his name as she rocked him to sleep in her arms. How could his memories of her be sweet?

"No," he roared. "I'm Bog."

"I can't believe it. You're alive?" She smiled briefly before her skin flushed. "He said that some rogue forest trolls killed you while I was in town. That liar! That monster!" Her neck muscles corded, eyes slit, lips curled back. "This isn't over," she hissed. "I'll trap him. And when I do—"

"No." Bog snarled. Not Jeddal. This had to stop.

"He stole you from me. All those years—lost."

With her mouth twisted and her eyes shooting fire, she was the monster, not Jeddal.

"You've hurt enough trolls!"

"Don't you see? He kept us apart! He did this to us!" His mother's smile was cruel. "Now, give me the Nose Stone."

"I told you, I don't have it." Bog crouched, ready to jump at her. Then he sensed movement behind him. Was Small about to attack him? After all, Bog was a liar.

He spun around. A shadow flitted over him. Small was soaring flat out, turning to stone already, his tail a flag of courage. Before Bog could try to stop him, Small fell onto his mother, using Bog's own strategy better than he ever could.

They slammed into the ground. A crash shook the forest floor, silencing the morning songbirds. Bog's mother lay on her back, her legs pinned under solid stone, her feet jerking.

"Small!" Hannie yelped. She crumpled against his side, at his mother's feet.

Bog couldn't speak.

His head screamed.

Small lay slantwise across his mother's stomach and legs, staring blindly at the rocky ground. His arms were by his sides; he hadn't even tried to cushion his fall. Above him, his tail was a stony plume, fur quivering as if it might crumble into dust at any moment.

"Get...it...off," his mother moaned. She rose on

one elbow and struggled to pull free of Small's bulk. When she couldn't budge, she collapsed backward.

"Oh, Small!" Bog bent down and stroked the rocky tufts of fur on the back of Small's head. If only his mother hadn't confronted them. If only she hadn't come after Hannie and the Nose Stone.

His mother lifted her head to peer at him over Small's shoulder. "Patrick. Help me," she pleaded.

"Don't talk to me." Bog growled.

"But I'm your mother!"

"Don't call for help. Don't move. If you try to break off one piece of him, you'll regret it." Bog steeled himself against her. Small knew he was half human, and he still honoured his *gnark*. Bog had to keep him safe until the moon rose.

The sun was a burning disk against a piercing blue sky. Hannie was still weeping. Bog watched his mother's eyes fill with pain and then close. Her hands went limp.

Bog circled Small to stand next to his mother's head. Then he crouched down, watching her chest swell with each breath.

He should silence her for good.

Destroy the Troll Hunter, just like he set out to do so many moons ago.

But he turned away, shaking.

He might be a fool, but he wasn't a monster. Not like her.

He crossed into the shade. He collected his rucksack from the leafy mulch where he'd dropped it. He felt for the Nose Stone, safely wrapped in cloth. Then he headed back into the clearing. He couldn't help flinching when the sun's rays hit him again.

Bog dug a length of cedar-bark twine from his rucksack and bound his mother's wrists together, hating the feel of her furless hide. Then he pulled Hannie off Small, and retreated a few paces.

"We can help him." He stroked her hair. "We'll guard him all day." Endure the company of his mother. "When the moon rises, we'll revive him with the Nose Stone."

"Small would like that." Hannie whimpered, her tears steady.

Bog nodded, holding her close, her slight weight like nothing in his arms. As the sun brightened, he calculated when the moon would rise. He sat back on his haunches, watching the undergrowth for any sign of humans and keeping an eye on his mother.

17

SUNWALKER

THE daylight blinded.

Slivers of sunlight trapped on dew-dropped grasses were like quartz cutting into Bog's eyes. Tears dampened his cheeks.

Bog squatted in the clearing, only about three hundred paces from the human settlement, his back to the broken statue that had once been Hornel. The forest leaves were a staggering display of green. Startlingly red raspberries dotted the thickets. His muscles twitched. Sweat streamed under his fur against his hide.

He fought the urge to flee to the shadows. Instead, he kept a wary eye on his mother, still passed out under Small, probably stunned by the blow when she fell. He half-expected her to rouse, break her bindings, hurl Small's weight off her, and come raging at him.

Or maybe a horde of angry humans would burst out of the forest, ready to kill. Was anyone wondering where the Troll Hunter had gone? She seemed to work alone, trust no one, and betray everyone.

He tried not to think about what to do with her once he revived Small—if he could revive Small. She was a vile creature. He refused to be like her. But if he let her go free, would she go after other trolls—after Jeddal's statue?

Hannie slept restlessly in Bog's arms, her damp clothing gradually drying. When she dropped her wooden troll doll, he returned it to the clutch of her fist. Her hands were tiny, with soft furless skin as pale as moonlight. Her closed eyelids were water-lily petals.

He missed the moon and the darkness. The flutter of bat wings, the muffled hoot of an owl, even the earthy scent of wood spirits. The daytime world was harsh and intense, with no friendly winking stars. Only the constant sun, its dry hot light forever pressing down, crushing him with brilliance, reminding him that he was a sunwalker. Not like Small. Poor Small.

Small had done what Bog couldn't do. He'd stopped the Troll Hunter. Bog owed him everything.

The sun climbed to the peak of the sky. Birds and daytime animals called out. Bog jumped at each noise, afraid the humans had found them.

When Hannie sobbed in her sleep, Bog rocked her,

letting her tears soak his fur. They were both cursed with hate-filled parents. He understood why Hannie wanted to escape her father.

Bog was endlessly on guard, exhausted yet fighting sleep, drifting in a haze of relentless tension.

Hannie's pale skin turned an angry pink, as if the sun's rays were burning her. He shifted her to a shady nest of leaves and adjusted his rucksack as her pillow. Then he put down roots right next to Small and his mother, easing the cramps from his arms.

Small remained a rigid statue across his mother, his long nose almost touching the ground, his mouth open as if to growl. Bog would have hauled Small free of her, but he was too heavy to lift alone. Bog checked his mother's bindings were still tight.

After the sun peaked, his mother's gravelly moan made him instantly alert. Her grey hair was fanned out on the rocky ground. Her nose was thin but longer than most human noses he'd seen. Her skin was leathery, brown, and wrinkled, with dark circles under her eyes. Up close, the three welts on her cheek looked like an old battle wound.

He twitched his tail back and forth, ready to pounce if she tried any tricks.

She twisted her wrists in their bindings. "Patrick," she groaned.

He stiffened. "I'm not Patrick."

"Is Hannie safe?" She lifted her head off the ground, wincing.

"Of course she is." He was surprised his mother cared. "She's always been safe with me," he said, which wasn't exactly true. But his anger at Hannie when he'd first met her seemed as ancient as the rocks he was standing on.

"Where is she?"

"Asleep under the maple." He waved vaguely in Hannie's direction, wondering why he was having a conversation with his mother when it was the last thing he wanted. "Now be quiet." He growled, as his mother strained against her bindings. "And don't try to damage Small, or you'll regret it." The stony tufts of fur on Small's tail seemed especially vulnerable. Bog wondered if she could shift Small sideways, jarring his tail.

Bog's mother lowered her head with a grimace. "I'd be tempted to snap off an earlobe if I could reach one." She stretched her bound hands as far as they could go, and Bog lunged closer, snarling. "But I won't hurt him, if you'll talk to me."

"I won't crush you into oblivion," he hissed, "if you shut your mouth."

"If you were going to do that…" she said, gritting her teeth as if a spasm had hit, "…you'd have done it long ago, Patrick."

"Stop calling me that!"

"I can't help it. That's who you are to me. Jeddal

and I could never agree on your name—or anything else."

Bog glared, watching her for any sign of movement toward Small.

"After all these years, you came looking for me." Her eyes were thorns, pointed at him. "Did Jeddal's lies finally ring false?"

"I came looking for the Troll Hunter." His fingers clenched as he remembered the stoning of Jeddal, and suddenly he needed his mother to know the hurt she'd caused. "Because humans, trained by the Troll Hunter, came hunting my family." Blood pounded in his ears. "Because they turned my father to stone. Because they would have hunted down the rest of us, even the youngsters, if I hadn't stopped them."

"So Jeddal is stone." A grin spread across her face.

Bog snarled.

Her grin faded. "You can't blame me for Jeddal's stoning. He started this fight when he told me you were dead."

"That's ridiculous." Bog's cheeks got hot. "So what if he lied to you? Is that enough reason to kill a hundred trolls? Or more? How many families have you destroyed?"

"You don't understand. I only went to town to get supplies." Her hands balled into fists. "We were out of bacon. It was your favourite." She spoke in ragged bursts. "Jeddal was supposed to be watching you. He was supposed to take care of you. But when I arrived home, he told me you'd been killed by a pack of rogue forest trolls." Tears filled her eyes. "He even showed me a mangled body that looked like yours."

Bog refused to be moved by her words.

"We fought for hours until Jeddal ran into the forest, tail between his legs." She spit out his name. "I cried for you." Her face reddened. "I arranged for your funeral. And I vowed to avenge your death. No other humans would suffer at the hands of trolls.

"At first, I dreamed about killing the rogue trolls and Jeddal, but I couldn't find them." She sighed. "Then I just destroyed any troll I came across. Eventually, I took up hunting mountain trolls since they were rumoured to eat humans. All these years of hunting, and now I find out that you were alive the whole time? This fight with Jeddal is all his fault."

"Jeddal was trying to protect me—his family— from you." Bog leaned closer, scowling. "Since you killed to destroy families, I guess he did the right thing." He leaned back, wishing for the moon to rise. How much longer must he listen to her?

She studied him in silence. Bog squirmed under her gaze.

"If you came to get revenge on the Troll Hunter," she finally said, "what are you waiting for? I'm trapped and helpless."

"Shut up." Bog ground out the words.

"You'd better do it soon. What do you think I'll do if you let me up? Give up my wicked ways and stop hunting dangerous trolls like Jeddal?" Her tone was taunting.

"He's not dangerous. And you'll stop," he replied, voice rising, "if you know what's good for you."

"Maybe I would stop hunting some trolls…" She paused.

Bog snorted.

"…if you'd promise to stay with me."

"What?" This had to be a trick.

"Don't go back to the forest." Her voice softened. "Stay with me, where you belong."

"You can't be serious. Why would you want to spend time with a troll?" He sneered. "We're only good for hunting."

"You're different."

"You know nothing about me."

"I know you've taken good care of Hannie—you actually seem to like her."

"Leave Hannie out of this."

"I can convince the other humans that you're not an enemy. First of all you're half human—"

"Half troll," Bog said.

"—and Hannie seems to like you, which will help. You also uncovered an illegal logging camp."

Bog shook his head, not sure what she was saying. "I *destroyed* a logging camp."

"Those loggers were clear-cutting the forest. You brought attention to them so that the police would know to shut them down."

Bog shrugged.

"And your fight with Hannie's father led to an investigation. The police began asking about

Hannie, and her teacher and neighbours told them their suspicions about her father. Because of you, James Vincent will be charged with assault and even locked up."

"Locked up where?" Bog asked, suddenly curious. Maybe humans did protect their young. If his mother was telling the truth, these *police* seemed fair and honourable.

Leaves rustled and a twig snapped. Bog glanced around, on high alert. Had they been discovered?

But it was only Hannie. She was sitting up, one hand clasped over her mouth, her pale hair tangled with leaves.

She scuttled over, gripping her troll doll by one foot. "Is it true? About my dad?"

Bog held out an arm. "Keep away from her, Hannie."

"Yes, it's true," his mother said. "And there's more."

"Don't talk to her," he told Hannie.

"The police located your aunt, Hannie." A smile crept onto his mother's face. "Your mother's sister."

Hannie gasped. Her cheeks flushed. "Really?"

Bog's stomach lurched. He wrapped one arm around Hannie and pulled her closer.

"Really," his mother said to Hannie.

"You mean Aunt Rachel, who made chocolate chip cookies and took me camping?" Hannie bounced on her toes.

Bog's mother nodded. "You can live with her when I bring you back." To Bog, she added, "If you stay with me, maybe you can see Hannie again."

"You're going to stay with...your mom?" Hannie's eyebrows lifted.

"No, I'm not." Bog jumped to his feet. "Now stand back." He swept Hannie several paces away. "She can't be trusted."

"I'm not lying." His mother raised her head, her neck muscles straining. "Your aunt's last name is Tremblay," she said to Hannie. "They found her in Winnipeg. Apparently your father refused to let her visit you anymore."

Hannie leaned into Bog's arm, straining toward his mother. "Where is she now?"

"She's in Strongarm, waiting for you."

"Stop lying to Hannie," Bog said. "It's cruel, even for you."

Hannie swiveled in his arm. Her eyes were large and watery. "What if it's true, Bog?" She clutched her troll doll. "What if I can live with my aunt?"

He opened his mouth to speak and then shut it. Could his mother be telling the truth? How could he be sure?

"Shush." His mother frowned. She tilted her head, listening. "Did you hear that?" she whispered.

Human voices. Southwest of them, maybe a hundred paces away. How had he missed them?

The humans were downwind. Coming closer. His eyes darted around the clearing, landing on Small, Hannie, his rucksack under the maple.

"Stay low," his mother ordered. "Don't move."

"Don't tell me what to do," Bog said.

But she was right. Running away wouldn't protect Small. And shape-shimmering only worked on objects. Bog pulled Hannie into a crouch and covered her pink rucksack. They sat as motionless as Small. His mother made no move to call out to the humans or signal them. Could she be trusted?

Bog strained to hear what the humans were saying.

"...can't understand why the Troll Hunter wants to...always running off..." a male voice said.

"I don't know, Larry. Who can figure her out?" another male replied.

Slowly, miraculously, the two humans walked farther away. Bog heard one loud bang, which made him flinch, and another. A car roared to life. Then the car moved off.

They stayed crouched for several moments.

Bog tried to stop shaking. Hannie huddled against his chest.

"You have to believe me, Bog." His mother finally broke the silence. "I would never hurt you."

"Why did you call me Bog?" He whispered.

His mother shrugged. "I suppose it's your name now."

He stared at her, unblinking.

"Now untie me so we can lift this megalith off me..." she said, a wave of agony crossing her face, "...and then get Hannie back to her aunt. I'll even help you revive your friend here, although I can't promise the same for Jeddal."

"But I don't have the Nose Stone—"

"Yes, you do. That's why you don't want me to damage him." She nodded toward Small. "You're a poor liar. Nothing like your father. I don't know what I ever saw in him."

Bog shot a protective look at his rucksack, lying under the maple. "I don't need your help." He was tired of the constant jabs at Jeddal.

"Oh, please, Bog? Please?" Hannie pleaded. "I'd like to see my aunt."

A quick look at Hornel reminded Bog what his mother was capable of.

"If the humans find me like this, they'll go after you. It'd be much better if I were standing, if I can. My leg may be broken..." she said, her forehead furrowing, "...but it wouldn't be the first time."

"I know," Bog said, remembering Kasha's story of how Jeddal and Martinique first met.

His mother raised an eyebrow.

"I don't forgive you for stoning trolls," he paused, "but it'd be easier to revive Small without you underneath."

His mother nodded. A smile tugged at one side of her mouth. "We could use a thick branch as a lever to lift him."

"As long as Small isn't damaged." Bog cut the twine around her wrists with his fingernail, hoping he wasn't making a deadly mistake.

18

MOONRISE

THE sun in the western sky finally brought some relief. The treetops blocked the sun, and Bog bathed in the shadows that fell across them.

Small was propped upright against a boulder now, after a tense hoisting with Hannie trying to help and Bog's mother directing the placement of the branch he used as a lever. He'd circled Small repeatedly, searching for a crack or a chip. Nothing. He could only hope that Ymir's life-giving powers would flow through the Nose Stone and revive his friend.

The air grew cooler as the shadows lengthened. The shade comforted Bog's stinging eyes, although with his mother still around, it couldn't soothe the tight knot in his gut.

Bog's mother was wrapping a strip of cloth ripped

from her sleeve around her left ankle. The ankle was probably sprained, but that was her only injury. She was almost as tough as a troll, which made him anxious and disturbingly proud at the same time.

Hannie sat cross-legged beside Small, stroking the stony tufts of fur on his foot and gazing into the distance with a dreamy look on her sunburned face. Her troll doll lay abandoned beside her.

Bog paced the clearing, pausing to check on Small every now and then. The moon would rise just after sunset—he'd spent all day calculating it—but waiting for moonrise was torturous.

When Hannie's stomach announced that it was breakfast time, Bog stopped pacing, realizing that they'd skipped dinner.

"You must be hungry," he said, even though he was too tense to eat.

"A bit." Hannie nodded absentmindedly. "Do you think my aunt remembers me?"

"Who could forget you?" He raised his nose, sniffing for nearby prey. A grouse pecked the ground north of them, but he didn't want to leave Small and Hannie alone with his mother.

"We have a few leftover deer mice." He slung his rucksack off his shoulder and rummaged inside it.

"Again?" Hannie made a face. "My aunt used to make me macaroni and cheese."

Bog raised his eyebrows and pulled out a jug of lake water. Maybe Hannie would be better off with this Rachel Tremblay—if she was worthy.

Hannie gulped the water. Her stomach groaned again.

"Why don't you pick some berries?" He pointed to the raspberry bushes that crowded the eastern side of the clearing. It wasn't troll fare, but he'd seen Hannie eating them before, when she thought he and Small weren't watching.

"Would it be okay, Bog?" Hannie's face brightened. "Trolls sometimes eat raspberries, don't they?"

"When they're desperate." He looked away so she couldn't tell he was lying.

"I like raspberries." She scooted over to the bushes.

Bog sipped from the jug, happy to see her smiling. As he swallowed, he realized how dry his throat was. Maybe he should eat, too. He'd need his strength.

He munched a roasted deer mouse, saving two for Hannie in case she changed her mind. As he watched his mother fashion a waist-high branch into a walking stick, his stomach felt no calmer.

Hannie returned with a handful of berries, her lips dyed red. "Try some, Bog. They're so sweet."

He wrinkled his nose. "You eat them."

Hannie's face fell, and he was tempted to eat the berries to please her. But before he could react, she zipped over to his mother, her hand extended.

"Do you want some, Missus…uh…"

"Call me Martinique." His mother's voice was raspy.

"Hannie, I told you to stay away from her," Bog

said, but his mother was already dipping into Hannie's palmful of berries.

Bog sighed.

"Okay, Martinique." Hannie smiled. "Bog has some deer mice, if you want. They kind of taste bad, but you might like them."

"No. Thanks." His mother shook her head. "I don't think he wants to share."

"Of course he does." Hannie yanked his mother up by the arm.

"Wait." She picked up her walking stick and struggled to her feet. With Hannie pulling, she hobbled nearer.

Bog packed the deer mice and the jug into his rucksack, scowling. "They're for Hannie—for later." He shouldered his rucksack and positioned himself between Small and his mother.

"Martinique is hungry, too, Bog," Hannie said.

"She can wait." He glowered.

Hannie looked from Bog to his mother. "But—"

"I'm fine." His mother stared him down.

"Okay." Hannie shared the rest of her berries with his mother. Bog watched his mother's jaw working as she ground the berries into mush.

When the berries were gone, Hannie said, "Martinique, when can I see my aunt?"

Bog's mother shot him a look, which he ignored. "When we get to Strongarm," she said.

Bog exhaled nosily and watched the shadows lengthen.

The forest grew dark and silent around the statues. The sight of Small and Hornel as stone was still a shock—Hornel with his severed fingers leaning against his feet.

When night descended, Bog dug in his rucksack for the Nose Stone. He wanted to be in position before the moon peeked over the treetops. He checked on his mother, who was leaning against a tree trunk about fifteen paces away.

"Don't come any closer." A rumbling growl built in his chest and throat.

"If that's what you want." His mother brushed her scraggly grey hair away from her face.

He wondered if she was really on his side—as if she'd help him rescue Jeddal. He retrieved the Nose Stone and unwrapped it, letting the cloth drop at his feet.

Hannie appeared beside him. "What do we do?" she asked.

"Small's father said to place the Nose Stone on the head of a stone troll while the moon is rising in the sky." Bog admired Small's determined expression, his prodigious nose.

Hannie looked up, her eyebrows bunched. "But there's no moon tonight."

"It'll rise soon."

Frantsum said a stone troll had to be whole for the Nose Stone to work. But what if he was wrong? Maybe the Nose Stone could revive any troll who'd been turned to stone, chipped or not. Maybe it could revive none.

Bog gripped the Nose Stone in two hands with the jagged side down and the curved side up. As he caressed the speckled surface, a tingle started in his fingertips and travelled through to his toes—a stirring of life within the rock.

He was infused with hope. Ymir had to make it work. For Small and for Jeddal.

Bog approached Small, with Hannie at his heels. He climbed the boulder that was propping Small upright and then placed the Nose Stone on Small's head with the flat side down so it wouldn't roll off. Although it looked like a crooked hat perched on Small's stony tufts of fur, Bog was awed by the sight.

"Please, Ymir. Bring him back." He held his breath for a moment before he climbed back down to stand between his mother and Small.

The moon glowed just below the eastern treetops.

Hannie slipped her hand in Bog's. "When will it happen? Is it working?"

He shrugged. "I guess we wait." He glanced at his mother, who gazed steadily back. Then he scooped Hannie into his arms.

They watched Small in silence. Bog willed him to change, to melt back into flesh and bone, to wiggle a finger. Something. Anything.

He wondered if Small would be happy to see him. How would Small feel about having a half-human as a friend?

The moon crawled above the trees, slower than ever. It was waning, just less than full with a blue-white radiance—Ymir's partly closed eye, gazing down on them.

When Hannie squirmed, they sat down to wait while Bog's mother rested against the tree trunk.

The eyes of a passing skunk flashed amber in the moonlight. Bog caught a whiff of a far-off deer. Forest life thrived around them, yet Small remained stone.

Bog's mother approached.

He jumped up to face her. "What do you want?"

She shrugged. "How long are you going to wait?"

"As long as it takes."

She studied a metal disk strapped to her wrist. "It's been almost an hour. If something was going to happen—"

"It'll happen." Bog clenched his jaw.

"It might not—" His mother reached for his shoulder.

He pulled away. "Don't touch me."

"Bog, I'm just—"

A crack sounded behind him.

"No," he moaned, sure that Small's fragile tail had broken off.

More cracks.

He spun around, bracing for the horror—just as Small's statue exploded.

Dust and rock fragments flew everywhere. Pebbles pelted them and rained down on the clearing.

"Small!" Bog shielded his face. His blood thumped faster than a woodpecker's beat.

Hannie shrieked. "He's falling to pieces!"

Bog blinked and wiped dust from his eyes. "It's your fault." He narrowed his eyes at his mother.

Then he heard a noise coming from the cloud of dust.

Coughing?

"Small?" Bog gripped Hannie's shoulder to steady himself. Jeddal could be next.

A furry arm, coated in fine brown dust, reached out from the cloud, grabbed Bog by the neck, and ripped him away from Hannie.

"Stay back, if you want him to live." Small squeezed Bog's throat, making his eyes bulge.

19

FAREWELL

BOG choked. Gagged. Clawed at Small's arm, desperate for air. Small hated him this much?

"Stop it! Small, you're hurting him," Hannie squealed.

She beat her fists against Small's side. Bog kicked at his shin. Small's arm loosened briefly.

"Quit fighting me," Small hissed in Bog's ear. "I'll get us out of here."

Bog's eyes rolled back. The stars spun.

Then Small said louder, "I'll kill him if you don't do what I say."

"You dove into the sun to protect him," she said, her voice low and throaty, "and now you're ready to kill him?"

"He's a useless half-troll." Small snarled. His tail whipped Bog's leg.

"Let. Him. Go." His mother spit out each word. "Now."

"Small, please…" Hannie whined.

Small's grip on Bog's neck relaxed.

Bog fell to his knees, gasping and clutching his throat. He wanted to scream at Small. Did he have to strangle him?

"Bog!" Hannie's face was in his, her breath raspberry-scented. "Are you okay?"

He nodded, unable to speak.

Hannie leapt to her feet, hands on hips. "Why did you do that?" She scolded Small. "You really hurt him."

"He was trying to fool me," Bog's mother said. "He threatened Bog because he knows that I care about him—that I might let you all escape rather than see Bog hurt."

Small gaped at Bog's mother. "How did you know?"

Bog rubbed his throat.

"It was obvious." His mother snorted.

Small shook the rock dust from his fur. He swiped the back of his hand across his face as if trying to clear his muddled thoughts.

"She's hard to trick," Bog said, his voice as gravelly as his mother's. "She knows how trolls think." He leaned on Small to pull himself up. "But thanks for trying."

"Thanks for bringing me back." Small tugged him into an embrace. As Bog inhaled Small's musky scent, hope for Jeddal's revival budded inside him.

Small pulled away, keeping a wary eye on Bog's mother. "It was horrible—listening to your every word, feeling an ant crawling up my leg, but being unable to move." He shivered.

"You could hear us?" It must be torturous for Jeddal.

Small nodded. "But you rescued me." He examined Bog's face. "You know I didn't mean what I said— about you being a useless half-troll?"

"I know now," Bog whispered, blinking back tears.

Small thumped him hard on the back. His bronze eyes were steady, warm, accepting. Bog couldn't quite believe it.

Hannie squeezed between them, smiling. "Can we go see my aunt now?"

Small furrowed his shaggy eyebrows and pulled Bog aside. "We can't let the Troll Hunter walk around free, even if she is your mother," he whispered. "And how do we know she's really going to take Hannie to her aunt? What if this aunt is no good?"

"I know." Bog shook his head. "One of us has to keep an eye on things." He and Hannie needed to go where Small couldn't follow. Into the sun. Into the world of humans. Bog shuddered, wondering what awaited him.

Small studied Bog and then nodded solemnly. "Will you be safe?" He glanced at Bog's mother.

She was leaning on her makeshift cane. With her thumb, she tapped on a palm-sized machine that had a glowing surface. Bog wondered what she was doing, although it seemed harmless enough.

"I think so." Bog shrugged. He didn't mention how nervous he was about going to Strongarm again, especially with his mother. Or about his plan to convince his mother to stop hunting trolls.

"Of course you'll be safe," Bog's mother snapped, looking up.

But would Jeddal be safe until Bog could get to him? Bog left Small and his mother cautiously watching each other. He rummaged through the rubble and dust until he found the Nose Stone.

"Are we leaving soon, Bog?" Hannie asked.

Bog glanced at the moon, which was still rising. "I'm going to revive Hornel first."

Bog placed the Nose Stone on Hornel's head and held back the branches of the fir tree so that the moon's rays brightened Hornel's hunched back.

Soon, Small and his mother wandered over and began tying back the branches. It was a strange sight, seeing them work together, and Bog wondered how his mother was capable of harming Hornel one night and helping him the next.

Hornel's statue glowed silver in the moonlight. Bog squatted in front, with Hannie beside him. They watched and waited.

Nothing happened.

When the moon reached the roof of the sky, Hornel was still stone.

Bog stretched his cramped muscles and rose to his feet.

"It's not going to work, is it?" Hannie asked.

Bog glanced at Small, who shook his head.

"No, it's not," Bog said.

Bog touched his nose to Hornel's stone one. Then he removed the Nose Stone.

"Small," Bog said. "Come here. Bring your rucksack."

Small retrieved his rucksack from the edge of the clearing where he'd abandoned it and then lumbered over.

Bog positioned himself so his back was to his mother and spoke just loud enough for her to hear. "You take the Nose Stone. Keep it safe." He winked at Small. Then Bog tucked the Nose Stone into his own rucksack.

Small hesitated and then nodded. "If you're sure that's the safest place for it."

"I'll come for it later," Bog said, hoping Small understood. He needed to keep the Nose Stone with him since Small didn't know where Jeddal was. He planned to duck out as soon as he could and head for Jeddal.

"Take care of her." Small gestured toward Hannie.

"You know I will." Bog and Small yanked noses. "Take care of yourself."

"You as well."

When Small yanked noses with Hannie, her bottom lip trembled. She sobbed and then leapt into his arms, wrapping her legs as far as she could around his waist and burying her face in his neck fur.

Eventually, Small untangled from Hannie. He cast a suspicious look at Bog's mother, holding her gaze for a long moment before he walked into the bush, heading north. Bog and Hannie watched until Small reached the crest of a hill and then disappeared. Bog bid him a silent farewell, imagining him returning home to Frantsum and the rest of the forest trolls, telling stories of their adventures and feasting under the stars.

"Let's go," Bog said to his mother. "Before I change my mind."

20

THE HUMAN MACHINE

BOG'S mother hobbled over roots and stones, leaning on her walking stick. She led them through the forest to a rutted dirt road. When Bog saw the car, as blue as the daytime sky, his heels dug into the earth.

"I'll never get in a human machine." The oil-and-metal scent burned the inside of his nose. He backed against a tree trunk.

Hannie gripped his hand and tried to tug him forward. "Please, Bog? Just once? We could get to my aunt faster." Her grey eyes were huge. "I'm tired of walking."

"I don't care how long it takes—" Bog stopped, thinking of Jeddal's statue, exposed and vulnerable. Could he reach Jeddal faster with this car?

"I'm not walking to Strongarm on a sprained

ankle." His mother opened a door to the car and a light popped on inside. "We can be there by midday." She gestured for him to climb in.

Bog squinted and looked away. The eastern sky was still dark, although the sun would soon rise. Could a car travel all the way to Strongarm—a distance that took days to walk—by midday?

Bog's mother edged closer to the open door. She re-adjusted her weight to her good leg and used her walking stick to reach into the car and press a button. The light turned off.

"How did you—" he began.

"Get in." She tapped her walking stick against his legs.

Bog glared at her and then climbed into the front of the car. His knees pressed against the ledge before him, which was dotted with mysterious buttons and dials. His mother's sharp scent combined with a strange plastic smell to create a sickening blend. She shut the door, trapping him.

Hannie scrambled into the back seat of the car, dropped her pink rucksack, and hung over the back of his seat.

"Thank you so much, Bog." Her voice was loud beside his ear. "I know you're going to love my aunt."

Bog's mother slid into the seat beside him and tucked her walking stick on the floor next to her door.

"I thought my aunt forgot about me, but now she's come back." Hannie was in such a rush to talk that she stumbled over her words.

Bog hugged his rucksack until he could feel the bulk of the Nose Stone through the leather. One ride in a car would be worth it to save Jeddal.

"She used to sing to me. I liked the song about the baby sleeping in the forest." Hannie's voice pitched higher. "I hope she remembers it."

The car roared to life and then jerked forward. Bog braced himself as his stomach lurched.

His mother pressed a few buttons. His window magically slid down a crack. It startled him, but he was grateful for the fresh air.

Trees began to slide by, rushing faster as the car gained speed.

"Oooh." He held his stomach. Closing his eyes only made it worse.

"Bog?" Hannie said. "What's wrong?"

He pointed to the rapidly moving earth, sky, and forest.

"But it's like flying." Hannie spread her arms wide.

Their pace increased alarmingly when they turned onto a road paved smooth with tar and stone. Bog pressed against the window and stared at the blur of trees, rocks, and sky until his eyes watered. The whole car shook. He wondered what kind of magic could make a machine go so fast.

Eventually, Hannie fell asleep in the back seat, her belly rumbling. The car swayed over the bumps in the road, carrying them closer to Strongarm. When the sun rose, Bog squinted, twisting in his seat to face away from the light—toward his mother.

Bog's mother reached into a compartment between them.

"Put these on." She held out a plastic object.

"I don't want it." Bog pushed it away.

"Don't be a fool." She held them over his eyes.

The blinding sunlight dimmed.

"You made the dark come!" He felt the thing on his face.

"They're sunglasses. They filter the sun's rays. You used to adore them when you were little." She showed him how to hook the sunglasses over his ears.

Bog didn't want to wear anything human, but these sunglasses were wonderful.

He stared past his mother out the window, watching the land and sky fly by faster than he thought possible. They passed under shady cliffs of ancient rock and then burst back into the light that blinded him in spite of the sunglasses. Bog was exhausted by the constant motion, the hum of the car, and the assault of sunlight, but he couldn't sleep with his mother around.

He watched her push pedals on the floor with her good foot. She seemed to be guiding the car around corners with the wheel in front of her. Although he was curious about how the car worked, he had more important questions for her.

"Tell me about the police," he said.

His mother smiled. "What do you want to know?"

"Do they shut down all the logging camps?"

"No. Only the illegal ones."

The car went over a bump. "Illegal." Bog held his stomach. "What does that mean?"

"It means against the law."

Bog wrinkled his nose, confused.

"We have rules—called laws—that everyone must follow. Humans are allowed to log, but the laws state how much anyone can cut at once in any one area. The logging camp you found was operating against the law. If anyone breaks a law, they can be arrested by the police."

"Arrested means captured?"

"Sort of. People who break the law may have to pay a fine or go to jail."

"Like Hannie's father? You said he'll be locked up."

"Yes. Why do you care about all this?"

He ignored her question. "Do the police have laws about killing humans?"

"Of course." She snorted.

"Do they have laws about killing trolls?"

Her face reddened. "No."

"Maybe they should."

His mother was silent for a moment. Then she said, "Bog, I care about you. I want you to—"

"If you care about me, you'll never hunt another troll again, especially Jeddal, and you'll stop teaching other hunters how to destroy us." Bog's nostrils flared.

His mother's knuckles went white on the wheel.

"Forget about trolls. I'm your family now. You should stay with me."

"Never."

"But, Bog, you can walk in the sun! You don't belong in the shadows. Hannie belongs with humans, and so do you."

Bog shook his head and stared stonily out the front window.

The car slowed. The squeal of grinding metal cut through his head.

He covered his ears, but Hannie didn't even wake up. "Why are we slowing down?"

"There's a restaurant up ahead. Even if you don't want to come in, you'd better put on some clothes."

He grimaced. "I'll stay in the car." He pulled on a hooded shirt. Once again, he needed to hide who he was.

When the car stopped, Bog nudged Hannie, relieved to have an excuse to wake her.

"Bog? Are we there yet?" She was groggy with half-open eyes.

"We're getting some food," he said. "What do you want?"

Hannie perked up, rattling off a list.

"I'll see what I can do," his mother said. Then she asked Bog, "And you?"

He hunched low in his seat, wary of the parked cars around them. "Not hamburgers." His stomach was still queasy. He doubted he could eat anything.

"I think I know what to get you." His mother

turned off the car and headed into the restaurant.

A few minutes later, she was back with silver containers for each of them. Hannie squealed. The car filled with a mix of smells, but the salty scent coming from Bog's food made his mouth water.

He inhaled, feeling the tug of distant memories. It was a scent he recognized. Somehow, he even knew the name.

Bacon.

His head began to spin, unraveling memories of his mother. A warm room filled with delicious smells. Bacon sizzling in a pan. The floral smell of his mother's hair. How had she developed that sharp, biting odour?

Bog was woozy with scent-memory. Who was his mother, really?

He remembered looking over Jeddal's shoulder, bouncing as his father walked. Leaving the cabin they'd shared with his mother. Crying out for her. Devastated at the loss of her.

"Why aren't you eating your bacon?" she asked. She was driving with one hand, and eating some kind of bread with the other. "Don't you like it?"

Bog's stomach growled. The bacon smelled delicious.

He took a large crunchy bite.

The salt melted against his tongue.

His mother smiled.

After Bog ate, sleep took him. He tried to resist, but his eyes fluttered closed.

He woke to Hannie shaking his shoulder. "Bog, wake up, please," she pleaded, her voice hushed.

He jumped, and his knees hit the front ledge of the car. "What's wrong?" The smell of gas overpowered him. His mother's seat was empty, the car's hum had finally ceased, and they were parked outside a white building beside the forest-lined road. "What is this place?"

"A gas station," Hannie whispered. "Listen. Martinique is outside, filling the car with gas." She pointed to the rear of the car, where his mother was pushing buttons on a machine attached to a hose. "We don't have much time."

"What is it?" The worry in Hannie's voice made him twist around to see her face.

"We both fell asleep for a while." Her eyes darted to his mother and back. "When I woke up I saw your mother going through your rucksack."

Bog's throat constricted. "The Nose Stone?" He yanked his rucksack open and rummaged inside.

"She put it in the big side pocket of her coat." Hannie frowned. "But I got it back without her noticing." She pulled the Nose Stone out from behind her back.

Bog grabbed the Nose Stone before his mother

could see. He ground his teeth. Jeddal's life depended on this stone—his mother knew that. How could she bring Bog bacon one moment and betray him the next?

"You did well." Bog shoved the Nose Stone into his rucksack. "Now we have to get out of here."

"I can't." Hannie's face tightened.

"What? Why not?"

"I need to see my aunt." Her eyes welled with tears. "I remember how nice she was, and I just have to find out…" She trailed off.

"Find out what?"

"If she loves me." Hannie's face radiated hope.

Bog's throat clogged so he couldn't speak. His eyes misted.

"But what if my mother doesn't take you to your aunt?" His voice cracked. "What if she—"

"I have to try. Please, Bog," she pleaded.

They stared at each other until Bog nodded. Hannie threw her arms over the back of his chair and hugged him.

"You know that I have to go?" His voice was gentle. "Take the Nose Stone and rescue my father?"

"Yes." She trembled. "Jeddal."

Bog buried his nose in her hair, locking her scent into his memory.

When they pulled apart, he said, "My mother will try to follow me."

Hannie blinked back tears. "I'll make her take me to my aunt first so you can have a head start."

"That would help." He paused, then added, "Are you sure you want to stay?" He didn't know what he was offering her. A life as a troll? Would his family accept her? Would Hannie even want that life?

"Yes." Her eyes were steady. "I think...I may be a human after all."

"Maybe." Bog nodded. "But you'd still make a good troll."

She smiled. "You should go before she pays. She can't leave without paying. That's stealing."

"Thanks." Bog yanked her tiny nose, wondering if he'd ever see her again, hoping she'd be safe, hoping her aunt would adore her as much as he did. Then he slipped out of the car, not caring if his mother noticed.

Outside, his mother had connected a hose from the machine into an opening on the car. Waves of gas fumes wrinkled the air. Bog's nose twitched at the scent.

"Where are you going?" Her voice was gruff.

He didn't answer. Instead, he moved fast and low, weaving between the parked cars and gas machines, avoiding the staring humans.

Hannie jumped out of the car and planted herself in front of his mother.

"When can I see my aunt? Call I use your cell phone to call her? How much farther to Strongarm?" Hannie assaulted her with a barrage of chatter.

"Bog!" his mother called. "Come back." Her voice

had a desperate pitch.

He raced across the highway without a backward glance.

"Bog, please!" his mother yelled. "I can't lose you again."

Bog kept running. His scent-memories of her might be sweet, but she'd never stop hating Jeddal.

He plunged into the cool green of the forest on the other side of the highway. When the undergrowth thickened, he ripped off the hooded shirt, leaving it under a pile of rotting leaves. He tucked the sunglasses into his rucksack.

After he covered his tracks by wading through a forest stream, he aimed for the clearing where Jeddal waited to be freed. It was maybe two days and nights of walking. With his mother on his tail, he'd have to do it in less.

21

THE CLEARING

THROUGHOUT the day and into the night, Bog sniffed the breeze for his mother's scent, but if she was following him, he couldn't smell her. When day broke, he put on his sunglasses, thinking about her stealing the Nose Stone and his confusing scent-memories. Maybe she hated Jeddal more than she cared for Bog.

He found a hole to sleep in when the sun was at its hottest. He should have pushed on, but he couldn't go another step without a quick meal and a rest. As the sun beat down, he caught a few fish in a lake dotted with lily pads.

Bog ate in a hurry, saving a little for later. When he packed the remaining fish in his rucksack, he discovered Hannie's troll doll. Maybe Hannie didn't need it any more. Or maybe she thought Bog needed it more.

He lay down to sleep with the doll beside him that day, pondering what it meant to be human and what it meant to be troll. Once he'd known, but now he wasn't so sure.

On the third evening of walking, Bog recognized a hump of rounded rocks with crevices lined with lichen. The sun was just setting, casting brilliant streaks of pink across the sky. Nearby, where a thick-leafed creeper fanned over the rocks, he and Jeddal had once discovered a warren of hares.

Bog picked up his pace, estimating that the moon would rise just after the stars speckled the sky. If he moved fast, he should reach Jeddal before moonrise.

He hadn't smelled a human since yesterday, so he was fairly certain no one was on his trail. Still, he kept his nose to the wind, in case anyone approached.

As he neared the clearing, Bog had a sudden dread that he'd find Jeddal's statue cracked, but he forced the thought aside and hurried on.

When Bog stepped through the cedars into the clearing, he was out of breath and his side ached. Starlight danced across the open space, lighting the low scrub bushes and the rocky ground. The large bulk of Jeddal stood where Bog had left him, still smelling of stone.

"I'm here, Father." He rushed over, hoping Jeddal

could hear him. How horrible to be trapped in stone, caught between life and death.

Jeddal was covered with bits of leaves, twigs, and even bird droppings. Bog's hands shook as he brushed Jeddal off, searching for any chips or breaks.

None. Not that Bog could see anyway. He checked twice, his heart thudding. Jeddal seemed unharmed. Bog sighed, although his stomach remained clenched.

Soon, the eye of Ymir would show itself. The giant eye that would bring Jeddal back to life. It would happen. It had to happen.

He dug the Nose Stone from his rucksack, thinking of Small and Hannie. He planned to tell Jeddal about them—how a forest troll and a human girl had helped a half-breed. Bog could almost picture the telling. Maybe Jeddal could meet Small and Hannie one day.

An owl hooted, startling Bog. He glanced at the treetops where the moon would first appear, checking for a tentative glow, but the sky was still dark. Gingerly, he stretched up to place the Nose Stone on Jeddal's head. He rubbed his nose against Jeddal's stone one and stared into his fierce eyes, willing them to move. Then he squatted on his haunches. He had to believe that Ymir's magic would wake within the Nose Stone and right what was wrong.

Only a few clouds dotted the sky. The tops of the trees began to glow white with moonlight, brightening Jeddal's nose and cheek, leaving one side of his face and his eyes darkened.

Still in a crouch, Bog waited, willing Jeddal to move, until the moon rose above the trees and then higher among the stars.

Jeddal was still stone.

"It can't be," Bog muttered. By the power of Ymir, this had to work.

Bog kneeled on the rocky ground, his eyes never leaving Jeddal.

Maybe it was because the moon was waning. Or because Ymir's eye was only half open. Maybe the moon needed to be full. Maybe the moon had to be higher in the sky.

"I'll try every night," he promised Jeddal. "When Ymir's eye is wide open and when it's closed. When clouds blind the moon and the sky cries with rain." He lowered his eyes, whispering now. "I'll never give up."

Bog slumped.

A crack sounded.

He jumped to his feet.

More cracks, crowded together.

Bog whooped, not caring who or what heard.

Hairline fractures snaked over Jeddal as if they were alive, widening into larger cracks. Bog worked his fingernail into a gap on Jeddal's chest and pried a section loose.

A small, flat rock flipped off. Underneath was grey fur, and a small dot of greenish-red blood where Bog had sliced too deep with his fingernail.

"Father?" He'd never been so happy to see Jeddal's blood.

The statue was splintering apart now. Rock tumbled around Bog's feet, and he stepped back, grinning. Odin's curse may have turned Jeddal to stone, but Ymir's promise could bring him back.

A burst of rock and dust forced Bog to shield his eyes. When he could look again, Jeddal stood—furry, dusty, and blinking.

"Father!" Bog squealed like a youngster.

He rushed forward and received a cuff to the head.

"That's for cutting my chest." Jeddal growled.

Bog laughed, and they wrestled until the struggle became a tight embrace. They fell apart, grinning.

"I don't know how you did it, son." Jeddal flicked Bog with his tail. "But you always were a clever troll."

Bog's cheeks hurt from smiling. Just being with his father, wrestling with him, felt so right, even if Jeddal seemed less agile than before. Bog hoped he'd enjoy the honour of old age, just like Mithanen had.

"I've so much to tell you," Bog began, picking up the Nose Stone from the rubble.

"Does it have anything to do with that fresh scar on your nose?" Jeddal said admiringly.

Bog nodded. It was agony—wanting to share everything at once but not knowing how to start. He had so many questions.

Jeddal stilled him with a look. His fur bristled. "I know that smell," he whispered. His tail twitched.

Bog sniffed the air and then stiffened. His mother! How could he be so careless? He should have been smelling for her.

He shoved the Nose Stone into his rucksack, cursing. "It's my fault..." he began. He hoped Hannie was safe.

Bog's mother pushed her way through the brush into the clearing, leaning on her walking stick for support. Jeddal snarled and cast a protective arm across Bog's chest.

"I've finally found you, Jeddal," she said in troll talk. Her face hardened. "And our son."

The fur on Bog's back prickled. "Don't hurt him." He growled.

"You know her?" Jeddal glanced at Bog.

"We've met. She's been hunting trolls. So much has happened..." How could Bog explain how dangerous she was?

His mother glared at Jeddal. "You taught our son to hate humans, even his own mother. You failed him in so many ways. He belongs with me now."

"Never." Jeddal's body went rigid, poised to jump at her.

"I'm not asking for your permission." She dropped her walking stick. "He's coming with me."

"You'll have to kill me first!" With a deafening roar, Jeddal dove for her.

"No!" Bog bellowed, plunging after him.

22

INTO THE FRAY

BOG'S mother whipped out a tube-shaped lantern and switched it on, blasting a beam of light into Jeddal's face. With an unearthly yell, Jeddal threw one arm over his eyes. Bog's mother shuffled aside, and Jeddal landed on his stomach in the rocks and dirt, his tail crumpled.

Bog smacked the lantern out of her hand, his eyes burning from the glare. The lantern rolled on its side, casting an eerie light onto the rocks.

"I told you not to hurt him." Bog helped Jeddal up, his arms shaking. He'd only seen his father fooled by humans once before, and it had ended with him turned to stone.

Bog's mother laughed, low and throaty. "I'll only give him what he deserves."

His parents faced off against each other, with

Bog between them.

He glared at his mother. "He doesn't deserve to die just because you're angry."

"Angry? I'm more than angry." She balanced her weight on her good leg. "He faked your death! Stole you from me! How is that right?"

"Was it right to force us to live in a cabin for years?" Jeddal swished his tail. "To make Bog dress in human clothes? To refuse to let him hunt with me? You would have taught him to hate the troll way of life—to hate himself."

"I did what was best for Bog."

Jeddal snorted, pacing back and forth, snaking closer to her. "Then there was that early morning when we came upon a troll family in a forest glen. Did she tell you what she did to them, Bog?"

"No, Jeddal, you'll only feed him lies—" his mother began.

"Your mother," Jeddal snarled, "turned the two youngsters to stone, right before your eyes!"

"They were threatening Bog!"

"They only wanted to play!"

Bog's head spun. He didn't know who to believe.

Jeddal lunged for Bog's mother again.

"Stay back." Bog put a hand on Jeddal's chest and tried to push him away, but he just leaned in, growling over Bog's head at her.

"You have no right to judge me, Jeddal." His mother's arm flew to her jacket, and pulled out a crude knife with a yellowed blade. She pointed it at

Jeddal. "I protected Bog then, and I'll protect him now."

Jeddal laughed. "You once pulled a gun on me. Now a foolish knife?" He slipped sideways away from Bog, fingernails extended toward her.

"Stop it! Both of you." Bog tried to wedge between them again, but they wove around him.

"I'm no fool, Jeddal. But you may be." The lantern lit his mother's face from underneath, making her hollowed eyes menacing. "This is no ordinary knife," she said. "I fashioned it from the fingernail of a gigantic mountain troll, so it's strong enough to puncture even your hide. I've dreamed of destroying you for years." His mother slashed at Jeddal.

"Don't!" Bog gasped. He couldn't lose Jeddal again.

Jeddal ducked under the knife, twisting to swipe at her with his fingernails.

His mother jerked out of the way, stumbled over her walking stick, and then righted herself. She drove the knife toward Jeddal again.

"No," Bog wailed, jumping in front of his father. The knife plunged deep into Bog's forearm.

He screamed.

"Bog!" Jeddal howled.

His mother yelped and released the knife. "I didn't mean to…"

Pain spiked up Bog's arm in pulsing waves. Greenish-red blood oozed from the wound and dripped onto the rocky ground. He yanked the knife free, screaming again.

"Look what you've done." Bog brandished the knife at his mother.

She clamped a hand over her mouth.

"I always knew you'd hurt him somehow." Jeddal got ready to spring at her.

Bog swung the knife toward Jeddal. "Leave her alone."

Jeddal's eyes widened. He backed away.

Bog's arm throbbed. He felt light-headed. "When you two fight, everyone gets hurt—trolls, humans, total strangers." He threw the knife as far away as he could. It landed in the bushes beyond the cedars. He hoped no one ever found it.

"It's her fault—" Jeddal began.

"You both played a part in this." Bog cradled his bleeding arm against his stomach, trying to slow the blood with his fingers.

"But, Bog—"

"No, Father. You mated with a human and stole the child you had with her. Then you refused to talk to me about my mother."

"I was protecting you."

"From my human side?" Bog spit out his words. "I have a right to know who I am."

Jeddal glanced awkwardly at the ground.

"And you…" Bog turned to his mother. "You only care about revenge. How could you hurt innocent trolls—try to kill my own father—and expect me to see you as anything other than a monster?"

His mother frowned. Her grey hair lay plastered

against her damp face. Her neck muscles were taut ropes.

Bog swung his rucksack from his shoulder, keeping an eye on them both. "Odin's crime started it all," he said, rummaging in his rucksack for something to slow the bleeding of his arm. "When he murdered Ymir, he began the hatred, fighting, battles won and lost. When does it end?" He pulled out the cloth he'd wrapped around the Nose Stone and tied it over his wound, grimacing. "When will you stop fighting?"

Jeddal moved to help, but Bog pushed him away.

"I can walk in the sun," Bog told him, "so I'm not a troll."

Jeddal winced. "Of course you are."

"And I have a tail, so I'm not human," Bog said to his mother.

She scowled.

"I belong somewhere in between." Bog untangled his thoughts as he spoke.

"What do you mean?" asked Jeddal.

"I need to know both of my worlds—troll and human. And I need you two to stop fighting long enough for me to do that."

His parents traded cold stares and then looked away.

"Here's what I want to do," Bog said, before they fought again. "First, I want to go home. See my family. Heal my arm. I have a lot of questions for you, Father."

Jeddal nodded. "I have questions for you, too."

"Then I'll meet you outside Strongarm," Bog told his mother. "I'll come at the next full moon."

A low rumble sounded from Jeddal's chest. "No."

"I have to, Father. I have scent-memories of happy times with her. I need to sort out the truth. And see a human girl."

"Another human?" Jeddal frowned.

"You'll really come?" His mother kept her distance from Jeddal.

"As long as you stop stoning trolls and tell others to stop hunting them, too."

His mother's eyes narrowed.

Bog held his breath.

"Fine." His mother's eyes flickered to Jeddal before landing on Bog again. "The next full moon then."

Bog let out a breath, giving silent thanks to Ymir. "How's Hannie?"

"Who's Hannie?" Jeddal asked.

Bog ignored him.

"She's fine." His mother nodded. "She's with her aunt. You can see her when you come." She retrieved her walking stick and her lantern, which she aimed at the ground.

"Good."

His parents exchanged a final, guarded look. His mother broke away first.

"See you soon, Bog." She glanced at Bog's arm and grimaced. Then she headed south, the lantern casting bizarre shadows as she went.

Bog sniffed her retreating scent and then turned to Jeddal, grateful that he was warm flesh rather than cold stone.

Jeddal's nostrils flared. "I hope you know what you're doing."

"We have a lot to talk about." Bog cradled his bleeding arm.

Jeddal nodded, his eyes probing Bog's. "I'd love to hear your story."

They walked together through the scrubby bushes and out of the clearing, past the rocks and trees that Bog knew with his eyes closed. Bog sniffed his way along the darkened trail, under the canopy of leaves. For the rest of the night, they'd hike north to the lakeside cave where Kasha and the youngsters would be doing their chores. Bog couldn't wait until they caught Jeddal's scent.

23

FULL MOON

THE troll was solid stone. Her eyebrows were ridged into furrowed mountains. Her nose was admirably crooked. Her eyes challenged a long-departed foe.

Under the flickering starlight of early evening, she perched on a granite outcrop that extended into a lake just east of Strongarm. Only a windswept pine clung to the outcrop—it had not been enough to protect her from the sun's rays.

"She's not worn or weathered." Bog's fingers worried over the troll, feeling for the slightest crack or chip. A chill breeze scattered the last of the autumn leaves across the outcrop. He shivered.

"I hope she's whole." Ruffan brushed pine needles from her shoulders, imitating Bog's movements. He was an eager apprentice.

Bog nodded encouragement and then continued to examine the troll.

She had the bristled fur, plumed tail, and muscular stance of a cave troll. He imagined her leaving the safety of the trees for a cool slurp of lake water. Maybe it had been almost sunrise. The outcrop was long and narrow. Had she been surprised? Trapped? Was it his mother who'd forced her to linger in the sun? It had been four full moons since his mother had stopped stoning trolls, and he could still find them too easily.

"Can you bring her back, Bog?" Hannie wound her fingers into the sparse fur on his arm.

"Maybe." He'd learned not to get his hopes up. He couldn't always undo the damage his mother and her followers had done.

"'Course he can." Ruffan gave Hannie a friendly punch, sending her sprawling briefly before she leapt up to wrestle him.

The two tumbled over the rock. Ruffan gripped Hannie around her middle, pinning her arms to her sides. Hannie sucked in her breath and slithered free, yanking his tail before bounding away, crowing her triumph.

Ruffan rose, grinning. "Not bad."

Bog nodded, glad her wrestling skills were improving.

The moon cast the first faint light from behind the treetops. Bog fished the Nose Stone from his rucksack just as the scent of two trolls reached him.

His tail twitched. He scanned the edge of the woods, finding two forest trolls easily. He hoped they wouldn't pick up Hannie's human scent. He didn't want trouble.

"It's him! I know it." He heard one forest troll say. "I swear on the bones of Ymir."

"The Keeper of the Nose Stone?" the second troll added. "What a story this will be!"

"I hear he can walk in the sun. He even tamed the Troll Hunter. He must be descended from Ymir himself."

Bog shook his head, amused. These trolls seemed more interested in him than Hannie.

Trolls everywhere had heard about the Keeper of the Nose Stone, and some had sought Bog out, asking for help reviving a troll turned to stone. Bog refused no one, since the Nose Stone wasn't for hoarding. In between, he roamed the wilderness, hunting for trolls to revive. He'd found plenty near Strongarm, where his mother used to hunt.

"Do you think the Troll Hunter did this?" Ruffan glanced around, his chin trembling.

Bog ruffled his fur. "She stopped hunting trolls, remember?"

Ruffin nodded.

Bog balanced the Nose Stone on the head of the troll. The moon peeked over the trees, shining Ymir's light down upon them.

Bog shooed the youngsters back, hoping the magic would work.

As the moonlight pierced the darkness, Hannie, Ruffan, and the forest trolls stilled. Bog could feel their eyes on him.

The moon rose higher. It was mostly full, reminding Bog that tomorrow evening he'd have to meet his mother. It'd be his fourth full moon with her. He wasn't sure how he felt about that, but he forced all thoughts of his mother aside and focused on the stone troll.

Sometimes a troll would burst free of the stone all at once. Other times a troll would emerge slowly, like a grouse chick pecking out from an egg. With this troll, the stone began to flake off like chips of bark from an old pine. Slivers of stone fell, making the forest trolls gasp, and Hannie and Ruffan danced in celebration.

"I told you it would work." Ruffan yanked Hannie's hair. "Didn't I tell you?"

Hannie thumped Ruffan in the stomach and then leapt into Bog's arms. "You did it again, Bog."

"Did you see that?" One of the forest trolls whooped. "We have to tell the others."

They bounded off through the forest, arguing over who would tell first.

Bog grinned down at Hannie and then peeled her off so he could welcome this cave troll and collect the Nose Stone. Others would need its magic.

When the cave troll was steady on her feet, the youngsters and Bog returned to the cabin Hannie shared with her Aunt Rachel, who had moved back to Strongarm to be with Hannie. Their cabin was tucked into the pine forest east of Strongarm—close to troll territory, as Hannie had insisted. Although Jeddal and Kasha still wished Bog would stay away from Strongarm and his mother, they tolerated his visits to see Hannie.

Inside Rachel's cabin, they followed the sweet aroma of cooking meat to the kitchen, where Small and Rachel were making a late breakfast for the trolls and dinner for the humans.

Small visited whenever Bog came to Strongarm, and sometimes he brought Diama to see Hannie. He loved Rachel's kitchen; so far, he'd roasted chicken in the oven and fried ham on the stove. Tonight, Rachel had taught him to make something called pot roast, which tasted as good as it smelled.

"I'll have to make this for Frantsum." Small licked his lips.

"Just wait until you try meatloaf." Rachel's eyes shone.

Rachel had the same pale hair and grey eyes as Hannie. Small liked her because she was a good cook. Bog liked the collection of wooden troll dolls she'd carved with Hannie.

They talked late into the night, until Hannie and Rachel couldn't stay awake any longer. At sunrise, Bog, Ruffan, and Small tucked into the darkened basement for the day, while Hannie and Rachel got ready for school and work in town.

Bog fell asleep to the sound of Small's snores.

When he woke, it was late afternoon. He rose without disturbing Ruffan and Small. Hannie and Rachel weren't back yet. He ate some leftover pot roast and then tugged on a large shirt and bulky pants that didn't flatten his tail. He hiked out to meet his mother by the main road—where they'd arranged to meet just before sunset. Even though she'd vowed not to hurt any more trolls, he didn't want her near Ruffan or Small, especially during daylight.

The sun was just above the treeline, so Bog slipped on his sunglasses. His mother waited at the end of the lane, outside her car. Her grey hair was cut short now, and her smile seemed genuine.

They nodded awkwardly and said hello without yanking noses. Bog had learned that he liked most other humans better than his mother. Still, he was willing to meet her if only to prove that not all trolls lied like Jeddal had.

"Where are we going tonight?" He rubbed his arm where the scar from the knife showed through his patchy fur. It had healed, but it ached sometimes, especially when he was with his mother.

"I thought we could go to a grocery store," she said. Her eyes darted to his scar and then shifted away.

"That's where they give out boxes of meat, right?" So far, his mother had shown him a park, where humans went to explore a tame version of a forest, and Hannie's schoolyard at midday, where youngsters laughed and played much like young trolls. Bog was getting used to having humans around, although he was still jumpy near large men who smelled like Hannie's father.

"Grocery stores *sell* meat—you have to pay for it. They also sell vegetables." His mother grinned as Bog turned up his nose. "You could pick out what you want to eat."

"I already ate. Can we go see the police instead?" Bog had been curious about the police ever since his mother had told him about them.

"We could go to a police station. Why?"

He shrugged. "If I explain that trolls aren't a threat, maybe humans and trolls can share the forest."

His mother raised an eyebrow. "I don't know if the police have time to listen. They're busy enforcing the law."

Bog frowned. Maybe she didn't want trolls and humans to get along.

"But I have another idea," she continued quickly. "Why don't we talk to my friend who works for a news agency in Thunder City? We could maybe drive down there and share your story. She might put it in the newspaper or on TV."

Bog remembered the glowing box in the restaurant where he'd first seen his mother. He'd since watched TV inside Hannie's cabin, but he'd never seen anyone else he knew on it. "Would a lot of humans hear my story?"

"Maybe the whole world."

"You mean the whole *human* world."

"I suppose so." She nodded.

Bog opened the car door. "Let's do it." The city might be crowded and the car ride long, but maybe he could convince humans that trolls weren't the monsters his mother had made them out to be.

Bog's mother drove slowly so his stomach didn't lurch with the bumps. He pushed his sunglasses up higher on his nose and cracked open the window to inhale the crisp autumn air.

AUTHOR'S NOTE

These events take place north of Lake Superior in Canada. Although Thunder City and Strongarm are based on real places, some features have been altered to suit the story. The rugged wilderness north of Lake Superior includes vast forests, countless lakes, moss-covered rocks, and the towering remains of ancient mountains. The Sleeping Giant stretches into Lake Superior with the ruins of a flooded silver mine at his feet on Silver Islet. Boulders lie in pine forests as if thrown, rock formations look strangely like craggy old trolls, and large unexplained footprints appear in muddy riverbanks. These features have sparked stories about trolls and giants, like the Ojibway legend of the Sleeping Giant, which I have respectfully adapted. The tale of Ymir, Odin, and the origin of the world is based on Norse mythology.

ACKNOWLEDGEMENTS

Many readers helped during the writing of *Bog*, offering insights into troll behaviours. Thanks to Pat Bourke, Anne Laurel Carter, Lena Coakley, Patricia McCowan, Mahtab Narsimhan, Karen Rankin, Sarah Raymond, and Erin Thomas. I bestow upon each of you the title of honorary troll. You have truly learned to think like one.

It was a pleasure to work with the enthusiastic team at Fitzhenry & Whiteside. To my editorial duo, Cheryl Chen and Christie Harkin, I affectionately yank your noses. Not only did you "get" Bog, you helped me understand him better. A million thanks for your passion and dedication.

Thanks also to the Ontario Arts Council and the City of Toronto through the Toronto Arts Council, who generously provided financial support and encouragement during the writing of this book.

And finally, to my family—Paige, Tess, and Kevin—I offer up a jug of broth in hearty salute to your patience as I wrote and re-wrote this book. You sat in dark caves with me, debated troll habits, and left me alone to write. You are high-calibre trolls—each one of you—for which I'm forever grateful.